AMERICAN
BADGES
AND
INSIGNIA

AMERICAN BADGES AND INSIGNIA

by EVANS E. KERRIGAN

with illustrations by the author

THE VIKING PRESS

NEW YORK

To my wife

PREFACE

Since the early days of conflict and war, men have distinguished their types of arms and their ranks by special markings, or insignia. These are a kind of shorthand by which the soldier or sailor makes known his organization and his place within it. Insignia in the armed forces of the United States are various and numerous, and those who know how to "read" them can tell to which service a serviceman belongs, what rank he holds, and what skills he has. In this volume we will deal with the individual insignia of the armed forces of the United States rather than with organizational insignia, which could be properly studied under the subject *flags* and would involve subsidiary discussion of regimental flags and standards, company guidons, ship pennants, and the like.

Military insignia fall into several classes. Devices that reveal a man's personal heroism are known as decorations; his participation in specified campaigns is signified by medals. These subjects were covered in my book *American War Medals and Decorations*, and so we shall not deal with them in this work. Here we deal with aviation badges, marksmanship badges, and the like, signifying a man's personal attainments. This book describes the individual insignia affixed to the uniform or headgear to show branch of service; shoulder patches to denote army corps, or division; ranks and ratings of the services and regimental crests of the Army; and qualification badges of all the services.

Have you ever wondered why military men throughout the world pay so much heed to these insignia, why specifications for each device and directions for wearing it are drawn up so minutely and followed so exactly? Besides identifying individuals in connection with their organizations and positions of authority, these symbols build morale. Military and naval insignia, running the gamut from the least involved to the most intricate, create a fraternity which men of all services know from experience. These devices are sources of pride in oneself and in one's organization; from this pride springs a discipline of self which is the essence of respect for self, for service, for country. A man who wears the badge of the parachutist or the sleeve tab of the ranger has earned it by the training he has undergone.

General George Washington recognized the advantages to be obtained by color and symbolic form; he devised badges early during the Revolutionary War so that rank might be easily identified. Since the American Revolution, the number of insignia has multiplied, and their purposes have expanded. A complete history of insignia would parallel the history of naval and military progress; it would trace and reflect the story of American engagements upon sea and land and in the air, and would mirror advancements in the science of warfare — for example, new techniques are recorded in insignia such as the Guided Missile Badge, recently adopted by the United States Air Force.

Insignia of the United States Armed Forces closely resemble those of armies and navies of other countries. Those for each service have grown out of the particular needs of that service. Many of the original devices have been changed or made obsolete, but these also are illustrated, and discussed, in this book.

The largest single class of insignia for the Army is the distinctive lapel devices, often called regimental insignia. Because of the scope of this field, this book can give only a general outline of the subject, and can cover the shoulder sleeve insignia only in a general, broader scope.

This book would have been impossible without the assistance I have received. Foremost I must mention my wonderful wife, Betty Ann, who encouraged me by her work and assistance. I am grateful to my sister, Mrs. Elizabeth Fassig, for many hours of labor editing this material.

My thanks also to Lieutenant Colonel John H. Magruder III, Colonel F. C. Caldwell, Major David E. Schwulst, and First Sergeant Peter Rizzo, all of the U.S. Marine Corps; to Mr. Jack Hillard, Head of the Archives and Library Section, Historical Branch, U.S.M.C.; to Major Joseph M. Massaro and George Catloth of the Institute of Heraldry, U.S. Army; to Major R. F. Prentiss and Master Sergeant Tony Pia, of the U.S. Army; and to Miss M. C. Griffin, Head of the Decorations and Medals Branch of the U.S. Navy. Special thanks must also be given to Lieutenant Colonel C. V. Glines and Major Robert A. Webb of the Magazine and Book Branch of the U.S.A.F. and Miss Anna C. Urband, also of that office. Special thanks also to Lieutenant Colonel Charles Burtyk of the U.S. Army, Commander R. C. Boardman of the U.S. Coast Guard, and R. A. Chandler, Chief of Seamen's Services, U.S. Maritime Administration. Special mention must be made of Gilbert Grosvenor of the National Geographic Society, and of the Society for its assistance. Thanks also to some very close friends whose assistance was invaluable in the preparation of this work: Colonel Alfred Wason, U.S. Army (Ret.), whose knowledge of this subject is unlimited, and Leon Bart for his assistance on World War I emblems. Thanks also to Ron Shepherd and S. G. Yasinitsky, to John Lockard and William Wells of the Anglo-American Medallic Society; to the many members of the Orders and Medals Society of America; to Jack Golden and Alfred Abbott for their assistance with the Marine Corps emblems; and to members of the American Society of Military Insignia Collectors, whose assistance was appreciated.

To the many people who permitted me to borrow generously from their knowledge I am most grateful.

E.E.K.

CONTENTS

Contents

INTRODUCTION

THOUGH THE USE of distinctive insignia for the military dates from the days of ancient Rome (if we consider the varieties of uniforms as insignia), we are dealing here only with the use of insignia and their application to the uniforms of the United States.

We shall not deal with the many varieties of uniforms as such; however, an outline of their development is necessary to place the adoption and development of insignia in perspective. The uniforms of the United States military have evolved from adoptions of the styles of older nations, with modifications from time to time as dictated by local conditions and national sentiment.

Before the Revolution of 1776, the Colonial troops naturally followed the example of the British forces. Some exceptions, such as Rogers' Rangers, were considered Colonials. They were, in effect, a territorial branch or militia of the home government of England, and were uniformed as such.

During the Revolutionary War the uniform of the Continental Army was rather like the uniform of the French Army of the period, perhaps an effect of the alliance with France. However, state troops were still garbed in the uniforms of their particular states: dark blue with red facings for Pennsylvania, brown and buff for Connecticut, and black and gray for Maryland, to mention just a few. Some Continental forces adopted certain features of the uniforms of the Prussian armies of the period, owing to the services of the Prussian generals Von Steuben and De Kalb. After the establishment of the United States of America, our small forces adopted some features of the frontiersmen's dress, such as deerskin jackets and coonskin caps. They wore these while fighting the Indians during the early western expansion.

The original idea of the Founding Fathers was to have every able-bodied man receive some training as a soldier, and from these plans sprang the militia of early days and the volunteer forces that fought the War of 1812. The militia were once again uniformed largely by their own states and territories during this war. Each unit was uniformed in military dress copied from various armies abroad, with different trimmings and colors to distinguish the arms of the service.

Insignia of rank started with the officer class and developed gradually. The first rank, authorized in 1780, was to be indicated on shoulder epaulets, which indicated an officer.

The establishment of a small regular Army after the War of 1812 brought with it government uniform regulations for the regular Army. They were in turn followed to some extent by the state troops or militia, but there were still many different styles of uniforms in use through the Mexican War, 1846–1848, and up to the outbreak of the Civil War, in 1861.

During the Civil War (1861–1865), many crack regiments of the militia, or, as it came to be known later, the National Guard of the various states, had the most distinctive colors and cuts of uniform ever seen on the American military scene. These units came to be known by their uniforms and colors, for example, the "Richmond Blues," the "Red" and "Blue" Zouaves, and the "Grays" of New York. Many units on both sides went to war as gaily outfitted as they might have been for the annual ball. As a matter of record, the first battle of Bull Run (Manassas, Virginia), on July 21-22, 1861, looked like a grand outdoor spectacle, complete with an audience overlooking the battlefield. Each unit seemed to be trying to outdo the others in color and pomp. In fact, it must have looked like a small-scale world war, with many nations aligned against one another.

The great Civil War called such large numbers of men to the colors of the two contending sides that considerations of economy and clarity demanded that the service uniforms for each side be made of a standard color and style. Ultimately, the armies of the North wore blue, and those of the South wore gray. In each army, however, it became necessary to distinguish the branches of the services by a distinctive color for the trimmings and facings on the uniforms: yellow for the cavalry, light blue for the infantry, red for the artillery, and so on. This custom, incidentally, prevails to this day.

During a battle in the summer of 1862 a mistake was made by a popular general officer, concerning the identification of soldiers of his command. This led to the use of distinguishing marks, which were known as "corps badges." The adoption of these corps badges was proved to be a morale-building factor; the drives for unit identification, *esprit de corps*, and pride in organization became important factors in leadership, discipline, and efficiency.

The corps badge was, therefore, the forerunner of the regimental badges and distinctive shoulder insignia of today. The Army began to use corps badges officially during the Spanish-American War, in 1898. Afterward, steps were taken to bring the uniforms of the state National Guards into general conformity with that of the regular Army. With the granting of national financial aid to these state troops and the issue of government regulation clothing and equipment, all the armed forces of the country — regular, state, and volunteer — gradually came to wear the same uniform. The different types of troops were then distinguished only by the design of the buttons or by letters worn on uniform collars. This continued until our entry into World War I (1917–1918). In July 1917 the first shoulder patch made its appearance. The use of shoulder patches spread like wildfire throughout the Army, and a new method of distinctive identification was born.

To this point, we have dealt with the uniforms and development of the land forces, namely, the Army and the Marine Corps. The uniforms of the Navy underwent a much more gradual change.

During the Revolution, the American Navy consisted of merchant ships armed with a few guns, manned by the hardy seamen of the Merchant Marine of the Colonies. Later, men-of-war were built especially for the service and manned by commissioned officers and enlisted men.

Introduction

The British Navy was so large and powerful compared with that of the Colonies that warfare was carried out more or less by raiding — a hit-and-run affair. The American purpose was to destroy as much British merchant shipping as possible. This type of warfare was carried on principally by privateers, merchant ships specially armed and built for such tactics. These were granted letters of marque by the Colonial Government, which permitted them to carry the flag and prey upon the commerce of the enemy. Under such conditions there was no fixed uniform, although the officers frequently provided themselves with a uniform patterned after that of the French Navy, with which they were allied. The men wore any kind of clothing that suited their fancy.

After the Revolution, although the standing, or regular, Army went out of existence, it soon became necessary to establish a regular Navy. By 1812 a regulation uniform had been prescribed for the officers of the Navy, with corresponding insignia of rank, but the regular seamen were still allowed to wear any kind of clothing suited to their work. Long cruises, however, made it necessary for the ships to carry a supply of clothing for the members of the crew, and as a measure of economy and convenience these clothes were all made in the same style. This custom gradually brought about a certain uniformity in the garb of the enlisted personnel of the Navy. Thus it came about that the accepted sailor's uniform consisted of easy-fitting garments suited to the work of hauling on the ropes and working aloft on the rigging, masts, and spars of sailing ships.

From the very beginning, the traditional naval uniform consisted of bell-bottomed trousers, which could be rolled up easily and quickly when the sailors washed down the decks; the easy-fitting, loose-necked shirt, or "jumper"; the short overcoat; and the pea jacket, for winter wear. It is much the same today. The first hat in use was a wide-brimmed, low-crowned tar hat. This hat proved unsatisfactory at sea, because it "carried too much sail in a gale." The hat was later made of cloth, but it still proved impractical. The officers of the naval service fastened it up against the crown on both sides and crushed the crown together in a "fore-and-aft" line. This was for many years the dress chapeau, or cocked hat, worn with the dress uniform.

About the time that officers started to pin up the sides of their hats, the enlisted personnel adopted a loose-topped brimless cap, rather like a large beret. To give the hat a smart appearance during shore leave, it was fitted with a light ring, or grommet, to stretch the crown out flat; the result was the common flat-top dress hat. The white sailor hat common today started out as a work hat only, and was a strictly American innovation.

Originally, the uniform was designed for wear aboard ships driven by sail power; however, it has been retained up until these days of nuclear power.

In all countries of the world, almost all naval uniforms follow the same general color scheme. They are the so-called navy blue for winter wear and white for summer wear.

Two unusual features indicate how closely our uniforms follow the style of the British Navy. The black kerchief worn by British and American sailors alike was adopted after the Battle of Trafalgar, as an emblem of mourning for the great Lord Nelson, who was wounded mortally during the battle, on October 21, 1805. And the three white stripes worn around the edge of the collar were so placed to commemorate Nelson's three great naval victories: at Copenhagen, the Nile, and Trafalgar.

Though the naval service has had a variety of "ratings" since its inception in 1775, it was not until 1835 that the first rating badge as such was authorized for wear upon the uniform. These badges indicate a sailor's rating or job specialty aboard ship. Insignia of rank were developed slowly over the years. Distinctive shoulder insignia were used for the first time during World War II for the Navy. This book deals with the development of insignia of rank, badges, shooting awards, wings, and the like.

It is the author's hope that this book will prove valuable to all people interested in military history and the development of insignia of the armed forces.

PART I

Insignia of Rank and Naval Ratings

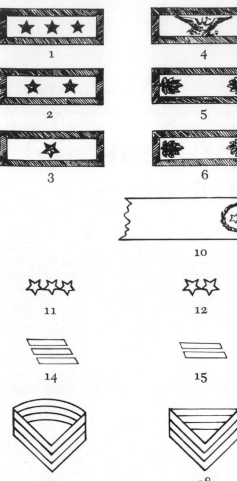

1

2

3

4

5

6

7

8

9

10

11

12

13

14

15

16

17

18

19

20

21

22

23

24

Aʟᴛʜᴏᴜɢʜ ɪɴsɪɢɴɪᴀ ᴏғ ʀᴀɴᴋ were first authorized in the Revolutionary War, there were as many variations in rank insignia as there were in the uniforms themselves.

General George Washington's order to his troops in 1778 stated:

> As the Continental Army has unfortunately no uniforms, and consequently many inconveniences must arise from not being able to distinguish the commissioned officers from the privates, it is desired that some badge of distinction may be immediately provided: For instance, that the Field Officers may have red- or pink-colored cockades in their hats; the captains yellow or buff; and the subalterns green. They are to furnish themselves accordingly. [As indeed they had to furnish everything, from uniforms to swords and horses, even food.] The sergeants may be distinguished by an epaulette or stripe of red cloth sewed upon their right shoulder and the corporals by one of green.

A few days before this order was issued, Washington directed that for the purpose of preventing mistakes "the general officers and their aides-de-camp will be distinguished in the following manner: The Commander in Chief by a light blue ribband worn across his heart between his coat and waistcoat; the Major and Brigadier General by a pink ribband worn in a like manner; the Aides-de-Camp by a green ribband." After issuing this order to field and line officers Washington directed that major generals be distinguished from brigadier generals by a "broad purple ribband" worn across the breast between coat and waistcoat. In these orders we see the beginning of distinctive rank insignia — before we as a nation had a uniform for all the services.

As we have seen, owing to the difference in uniforms worn by the various militia units, we do not really begin to find a series of ranks and distinctive insignia until the Civil War.

Distinctive shoulder insignia, which are still in use today, came into being in 1780 and gradually developed as the services grew in size and scope. To show completely the development of these ranks, it would be necessary to place it parallel to a complete history of naval and military progress, tracing and reflecting the story of America's growth and its engagements on sea and on land and mirroring advancements in the science of warfare.

In 1780, major generals were ordered to wear two epaulets, with two stars on each, and brigadier generals one star on each. In 1799, when the rank of lieutenant general was established, three silver stars were specified. In 1832, embroidered spread eagles for epaulets of colonels were prescribed.

In 1836, embroidered shoulder straps for field duty replaced the epaulets. New ranks were established at this time. Their insignia included gold-embroidered leaves for majors; captains were ordered to wear two embroidered bars; and first lieutenants were ordered to wear one. It is often asked why silver outranks gold in grade insignia for the military services. The answer to this question is in historical background. In 1832, an order had specified that eagles worn by colonels in the infantry should be gold while those for all other colonels were to be silver. When undress, or field, uniforms were prescribed in 1851, it was decided that all colonels should wear the same insigne, and that it should be the silver eagle. This was based on the practical fact that there were more colonels with the silver eagle insigne. This decision was also considered appropriate since generals already had silver stars. The 1832 order also created the rank of lieutenant colonel and specified that oak leaves of silver were to be the insignia. Thus all officers from general to lieutenant colonel had silver insignia. Majors used the same oak-leaf design, but it was in gold. At the same time, captains' and first lieutenants' bars were designated as gold, with two bars for captains and one for lieutenants. (These bars were redesignated as silver in 1872. In 1917, when the rank of second lieutenant was established, this single bar was made gold, and the rank of first lieutenant was signified by a single silver bar.)

The first uniform enlisted ranks — those of corporal and sergeant — were established in 1833. In 1847, the corporal's designation was two stripes, and the sergeant's three stripes. To this the ranks of sergeant major and regimental quartermaster sergeant were added. The sergeant major's chevron was the same as that of the sergeant — three stripes with a single upper convex bar. The quartermaster sergeant had three stripes, with a straight bar at the top. These stripes were quite large, 7 inches by 11 inches, and they covered the width of the sleeve area. They were worn inverted with point down. These stripes were added to during the Civil War.

This section begins with the rank insignia used during the Civil War by both the Union and Confederate forces; it continues to the present day. It deals also with some of the specialty ratings used by the Army up to World War II, and with the naval specialty rating and distinguishing marks.

CIVIL WAR INSIGNIA

DURING THE CIVIL WAR (1861-1865) distinguishing ranks were used by both the United States and Confederate States. As we have seen, epaulets were discontinued for the field uniform and were replaced by shoulder straps. This was the case in the United States forces, but in the Confederate States Army the insignia of rank were sewn directly upon the raised collars. The chevrons used by the enlisted men were almost identical in both armies.

The shoulder straps were woven in a rectangular shape, 5 inches long by 1½ inches wide. The background cloth signified the branch of service: light blue for infantry, yellow for cavalry, and red for artillery. The edges were woven of metallic cloth in gold color, and the insigne inside the border signifies the wearer's rank.

The following were used by the United States Army.

1. **Lieutenant General**
   Three five-pointed silver stars (center star slightly larger than others).
2. **Major General**
   Two five-pointed silver stars.
3. **Brigadier General**
   One five-pointed silver star.
4. **Colonel**
   A spread eagle, 2 inches wide, in silver.
5. **Lieutenant Colonel**
   Silver oak leaves, one at either end of the bar.
6. **Major**
   Gold oak leaves, one at either end of the bar.
7. **Captain**
   Two gold bars, in pairs at either end of the shoulder strap.
8. **First Lieutenant**
   One gold bar at either end of the shoulder strap.
9. **Second Lieutenant**
   A complete shoulder strap without any inner distinguishing insigne of rank. The color signifies the branch of service.

The following ranks were used by the Confederate States during the war. The color of the high collar signified the branch of service the wearer served in, and the following distinctive insignia, sewn directly upon the collar, signified the rank of the wearer. The same colors were used as in the United States Army — blue for infantry, red for artillery, and so on.

10. **General**
    One large five-pointed star, flanked by two smaller five-pointed stars. The whole, of gold, enclosed by a wreath of laurel.
11. **Colonel**
    Three gold five-pointed stars, aligned.
12. **Lieutenant Colonel**
    Two gold five-pointed stars.
13. **Major**
    A single gold five-pointed star.

14. **Captain**
    Three ½-inch diagonal stripes in gold.
15. **First Lieutenant**
    Two ½-inch diagonal stripes in gold.
16. **Second Lieutenant**
    A single diagonal stripe in gold, ½ inch high by 2 inches long.

The following chevrons were used by both the United States Army and the Army of the Confederacy. They were very wide, covering the whole width of the sleeve, about 7½ inches. The color signified the branch of service. These stripes, in the appropriate color, were usually separated by narrow stripes of navy blue or black.

17. **Sergeant Major**
    Three chevrons, point down, with three half-circular arc stripes above. (These are the reverse of the "rockers" worn today.)
18. **Quartermaster Sergeant**
    Three chevrons, point down, and three horizontal bars at the top.
19. **Ordnance Sergeant**
    Three chevrons, point down. At the juncture of the stripes is a five-pointed star with one point down.
20. **First Sergeant**
    Three chevrons, point down. At the juncture of the stripes is a diamond shape indicating rank.
21. **Sergeant**
    Three chevrons, point down.
22. **Corporal**
    Two chevrons, point down.

The following two ranks were worn only in the United States Army, though there were no doubt such personnel in the Confederate Army.

23. **Hospital Steward**
    A thin diagonal stripe with a caduceus design within; worn across the sleeve like a half chevron.

24. Pioneer
Two crossed woodman's axes.

ARMY, AIR FORCE, COAST GUARD, MARINE CORPS, AND NAVY INSIGNIA

THE FOLLOWING commissioned officers' and warrant officers' ranks are worn on the shoulder straps of the Army, Air Force, and Marine Corps uniforms or on the collar of the uniform shirt for all services. These ranks are sometimes worn on the helmet or field hat of the services in time of war or for field dress. Both the Navy and the Coast Guard use a special dress shoulder board, plus insignia of rank on the sleeve of the dress coat. On the field, or undress, uniform, personnel of the naval service also wear the same rank insignia as the other armed forces. In other words, for the Army, Air Force, and Marine Corps there is only one type of rank insigne, worn in various ways, depending upon the uniform. For the Navy and the Coast Guard there are three different styles of rank insignia, although in fact sleeve insignia are worn only on the dress uniform, along with the shoulder boards.

25. General of the Army
The pentagonal design consists of five five-pointed silver stars, all connected. Above this is the shield of the Army in gold and full colors. It consists of an American eagle with wings spread, gripping laurel leaves and a bunch of arrows in its claws. On its breast is a shield. The chief, or top, is in blue, with four white and three red stripes at its base. Above is a cloud formation in gold; the center is blue with thirteen white stars.

26. General of the Air Force
Five silver stars of five points, joined in a pentagonal pattern.

27. Fleet Admiral or **Admiral of the Navy**
The shoulder board consists of a wide gold woven board edged in navy blue. Within the board are five silver stars of five points in a pentagonal shape. Above this is a fouled

26

27

25

28

32

29

30

31

33

34

35

36

37

38

39

40

41

42

43

naval anchor, also in silver. The sleeve insigne is a wide 2-inch stripe of gold with four ½-inch stripes above it. At the top or above the stripes is a five-pointed star with one point down, also in gold. These stripes are embroidered, as are all the sleeve stripes of the Navy.

28. **Fleet Admiral** (**Collar Insigne**)
This is made up of five silver stars of five points each, joined in a pentagonal pattern.

29. **General** or **Admiral**
Four five-pointed silver stars in a line.
Commandant of the Marine Corps
Four five-pointed silver stars, joined. (Not shown.)

30. **Lieutenant General** and **Vice Admiral**
Three five-pointed silver stars in a line.

31. **Major General** and **Rear Admiral**
Two five-pointed silver stars in a line.

32. **Brigadier General** and **Commodore**
One five-pointed silver star.

33. **Colonel** and **Navy Captain**
An American eagle facing left, with wings spread, gripping arrows and laurel leaves. There is an American shield on its breast. It is all in silver.

34. **Lieutenant Colonel** and **Commander**
A sculptured silver oak leaf.

35. **Major** and **Lieutenant Commander**
A sculptured gold oak leaf.

36. **Captain** and **Navy Lieutenant**
Two joined bars of silver, 1 inch long by ¼ inch wide.

37. **First Lieutenant** and **Navy Lieutenant Junior Grade**
One bar of silver, 1 inch by ¼ inch.

38. **Second Lieutenant** and **Ensign**
One bar, 1 inch by ¼ inch, in gold.

39. **Chief Warrant Officer, W-4** (**All Branches**)
One bar of enameled color, broken by two crosswise bars of silver, and framed in silver. The color is blue for the Navy and the Air Force and red for the Army and the Marine Corps.

40. Chief Warrant Officer, W-3 (All Branches)
One bar of enameled color, separated by a centered cross-wise bar of silver, and framed in silver. The color is blue for the Navy and the Air Force and red for the Army and the Marine Corps.

41. Chief Warrant Officer, W-2 (All Branches)
One bar of enameled color, broken by two crosswise bars of gold, and framed in gold. The color is blue for the Navy and the Air Force and red for the Army and the Marine Corps.

42. Warrant Officer, W-1 (All Branches)
One bar of enameled color, separated by a centered cross-wise bar of gold, and framed in gold. The color is blue for the Navy and the Air Force and red for the Army and the Marine Corps.

43. Chief Marine Gunner (Marine Corps)
This rank is worn in addition to the warrant officer ranks above. However, it was once worn as a rank insigne. It is a sculptured bursting bomb, in metal or embroidered. It is bronze for the green and khaki uniforms and the field uniform and silver for the dress blue uniform.

The following are shoulder boards and sleeve insignia of the naval service. Sleeve insigne is worn only on the dress uniform — that is, the khaki and white uniforms. Shoulder boards are worn on the white and blue dress uniforms and on the blue over-coat. They need not be worn on the dress blue uniform, however; that makes it an undress uniform.

The stripes are embroidered gold on gold, and are either wide (2 inches) or narrow (½ inch) or a combination of both.

The same rank insignia are worn by the Coast Guard, but with these changes: on the shoulder boards of the admiral's and commodore's rate, the Coast Guard shield is shown superimposed upon the anchor. For all other ranks, the Coast Guard shield replaces the five-pointed star. On the sleeve insignia, the Coast Guard shield also replaces the star and is above the stripes.

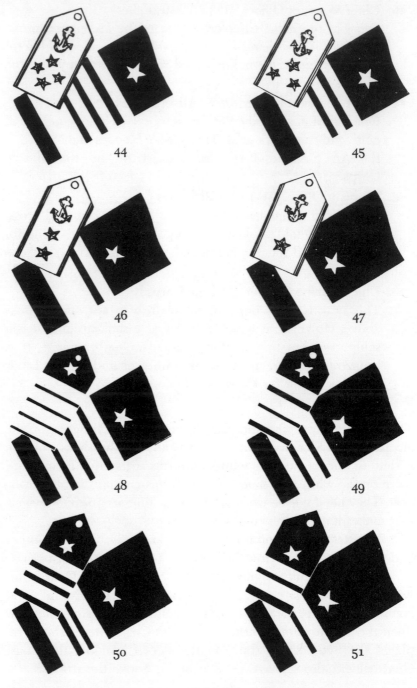

44

45

46

47

48

49

50

51

44. Admiral

Shoulder board: gold embroidered with navy blue edges at the lower half. It also has four embroidered five-pointed stars of silver in a diamond pattern with a fouled anchor of silver above. Sleeve insigne: one wide gold stripe with three narrow stripes above it and at the top, a five-pointed star with one point down.

45. Vice Admiral

Shoulder board: the same as the above, with three silver stars in a triangle pattern in the lower half. Sleeve insigne: one wide gold stripe with two narrow stripes above, and a star above that.

46. Rear Admiral

Shoulder board: same as the above, but with two five-pointed stars in silver, one star above the other. Sleeve insigne: one wide gold stripe, with a narrow stripe above it, and above that a star.

47. Commodore

Shoulder board: same as above, but with a single five-pointed star of silver. Sleeve insigne: one wide gold stripe, with a star above.

The following ranks are the same on the shoulder board and the sleeve.

48. Captain

Four narrow stripes in gold, with a five-pointed star of gold above them.

49. Commander

Three narrow stripes in gold with a star above them.

50. Lieutenant Commander

Two narrow, ½-inch stripes of gold, with a thin, ¼-inch stripe between them and a star above.

51. Lieutenant

Two narrow stripes of gold, with a gold star above.

52. Lieutenant Junior Grade

A narrow, ½-inch stripe, with a thin, ¼-inch stripe above it, and a star above that.

53. Ensign

A narrow, ½-inch stripe with a five-pointed star with one point down above the stripe.

The following insignia for the warrant officer grade have a pair of fouled anchors, crossed, in gold, in place of the five-pointed star. The insignia are the same on the sleeve and the shoulder board.

54. Chief Warrant Officer, W-4

A thin, ¼-inch stripe of gold with a narrow perpendicular light blue stripe in the center. Above this are two fouled anchors, crossed.

55. Chief Warrant Officer, W-3

A thin gold stripe with two perpendicular light blue stripes, one to either side of the center.

56. Chief Warrant Officer, W-2

A thin gold stripe with three perpendicular light blue stripes, one in the center and one to either side near the edge. On the shoulder boards they are at the ends.

These insignia are worn upon the hat or, in miniature, upon the lapel of the uniform shirt in the field.

57. Navy Commissioned Officer

A shield, with stars in the chief and stripes below. Atop this, in silver, is an American eagle, wings spread, facing left. Behind this is a pair of fouled naval anchors, crossed and in gold.

58. Navy Warrant Officer

A pair of naval anchors, fouled, with small flukes and long stems, all in gold.

The shoulder boards previously described were also worn on the gray uniform during World War II. On that uniform the stripes and stars were black. The same, or navy blue and gold, shoulder boards were worn upon the khaki uniform.

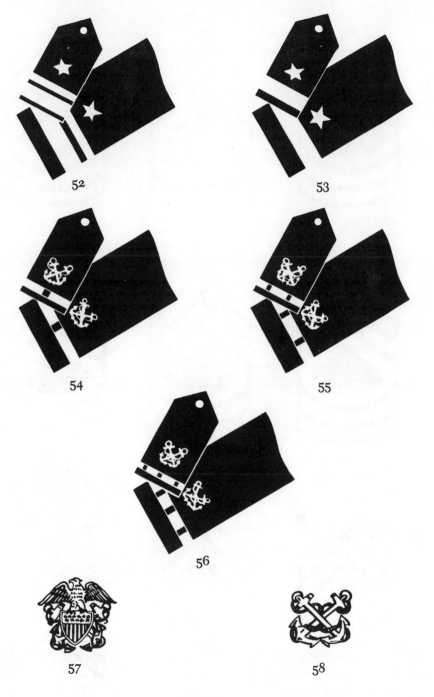

52

53

54

55

56

57

58

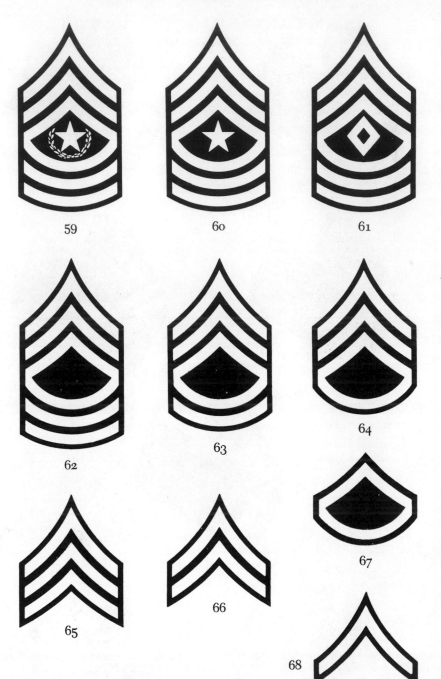

59

60

61

62

63

64

65

66

67

68

ARMY INSIGNIA OF GRADE
(ENLISTED MEN)

THE FOLLOWING are insignia of grade for enlisted men of the United States Army. We will illustrate and describe the patches currently in use, and though we will not illustrate the many changes that have taken place in this type of insignia, we will describe them.

After each title the pay grade of each rank is indicated in parentheses.

The chevrons, arcs, lozenges, and other designs are in gold on an army green or are in dark blue on a white cloth for the dress uniform of the Army.

59. **Sergeant Major** (E-9)
    Three chevrons above, three arcs below, with a five-pointed star completely encircled by a wreath of laurel in the center.
60. **Chief Master Sergeant** (E-9)
    Three chevrons above, three arcs below, with a five-pointed star in the center between them.
61. **First Sergeant** (E-8)
    Three chevrons above, three arcs below, with a lozenge, or open diamond shape, in the center between them.
62. **Master Sergeant** (E-8)
    Three chevrons above and three arcs below.
63. **Sergeant First Class** (E-7)
    Three chevrons above and two arcs below.
64. **Staff Sergeant** (E-6)
    Three chevrons above and one arc below.
65. **Sergeant** (E-5)
    Three chevrons, point up.
66. **Corporal** (E-4)
    Two chevrons, point up.
67. **Lance Corporal** (E-3)
    One chevron, with one arc below.
68. **Private First Class** (E-2)
    One chevron, point up.

During World War II, these chevrons were dark khaki or army brown on a navy blue background. All the patches except the sergeant major, chief master sergeant, and lance corporal patches were used, although the official designation was different. Technician grades were also used. These were indicated by a gothic letter "T" placed between the chevrons and the arc on the staff sergeant grade, and also in a half arc of blue below the three chevrons of the sergeant. This meant technician 4th grade, and when it was worn by a corporal it indicated technician 5th grade. The letter "T" was in the same color as the chevrons.

The following insignia are used in the Army to designate certain specialists' fields. They all have the same center design, an American eagle device in gold on an army green or navy blue background. They are a good deal smaller than the other insignia of rank.

69. Specialist Nine (E-9)
   The specialist center design, with three arcs above and two inverted chevrons below, point down. (No longer authorized.)

70. Specialist Eight (E-8)
   The specialist center design, with three arcs above, and below, one inverted chevron, pointed down. (No longer authorized.)

71. Specialist Seven (E-7)
   The specialist center design, with three arcs above.

72. Specialist Six (E-6)
   The specialist center design, with two arcs above.

73. Specialist Five (E-5)
   The specialist center design, with one arc above.

74. Specialist Four (E-4)
   The specialist insignia alone. It is arched at the top and shaped like an inverted chevron below.

75. Army Meritorious Unit Award
   This is a 2-inch olive drab, or army green, square with an open laurel wreath, joined at the bottom by a bow — all in

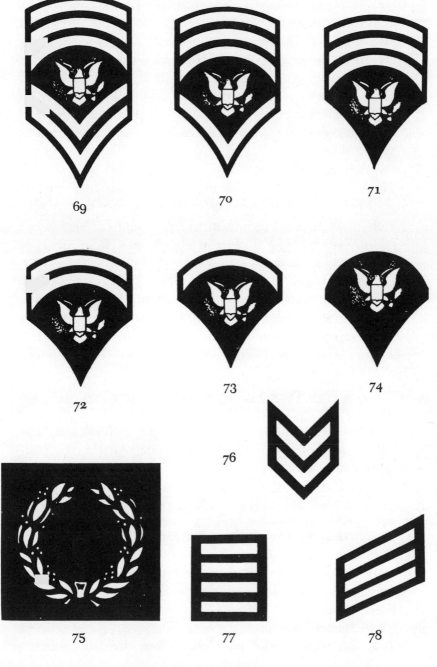

69

70

71

72

73

74

75

76

77

78

gold. This is authorized for wear by Army personnel attached to units awarded a Meritorious Unit Citation. Second, third, and fourth awards are indicated by a numeral, also in gold, in the center of the wreath.

76. **Overseas Chevrons, World War I,** and **Wound Chevron**
These insignia are worn on the outside sleeve, near the cuff. They are inverted chevrons, point down, of gold color on army green. One chevron is authorized for each wound or for each six months' service in a theater of operations during World War I.

77. **Overseas Service Bars, World War II** and **Korean War**
These are worn in the same manner as the above. Each is a gold bar on a background of army green. The bar is 1$\frac{5}{16}$ inch in length and $\frac{3}{16}$ inch in width. Each bar indicates six months' service in a theater of operations.

78. **Army Service Stripes**
Diagonal stripes in gold on an army green background, worn on the outside sleeve of the uniform. Each gold stripe indicates three years of federal military service, and they are worn one above another.

AIR FORCE INSIGNIA (ENLISTED MEN)

THE FOLLOWING are the insignia of rank for enlisted men and noncommissioned officers of the United States Air Force. (During World Wars I and II, the air arm was a branch of the United States Army and therefore wore Army uniforms and insignia.) These chevrons are silver-colored on navy blue background cloth.

79. **First Sergeant Distinguishing Device**
This is a lozenge, or open diamond design which, when worn above any chevrons, in the location indicated in the drawing, signifies the wearer as the first sergeant of an Air Force organization.

80. **Chief Master Sergeant**
Two chevrons at the top, and below this, six inverted

rounded chevrons, with a circular center design, and a five-pointed star within it.

81. Senior Master Sergeant
A single chevron at the top, and below this, the same six inverted rounded chevrons and center design as above.

82. Master Sergeant
Six inverted rounded chevrons. Within this is a five-pointed star on a circular disk of blue.

83. Technical Sergeant
Five inverted rounded chevrons; within is a five-pointed star in a circular disk of blue.

84. Staff Sergeant
Four inverted rounded chevrons; within this is a five-pointed star in a circular disk of blue.

On the following insignia, the center design is a circular disk of blue, with a five-pointed star in silver, within which is a center disk of blue. The first three insignia appear to have the chevron in back of the design, because the points of the chevron disappear into it.

85. Airman First Class
Three chevrons and the center design.

86. Airman Second Class
Two chevrons and the center design.

87. Airman Third Class
A single chevron and the center design.

The following two insignia, slightly larger and without the outer circle, are worn by the commissioned officers of the Air Force.

88. Enlisted Man (Cap Insigne)
This has the American eagle with wings spread and a shield upon its breast. Above it is the usual cloud design with thirteen stars within an open circle. All this is carried out in silver.

89. Enlisted Man (Lapel Insigne)
This has the letters "U.S." in gothic block form within an

79

80

81

82

83

84

85

86

87

88

89

90

91

open circle, all carried out in silver. It is worn upon the lapel.

90. **Overseas Chevron, World War I**

These inverted chevrons, silver on navy blue, are worn on the lower sleeve. Each one signifies six months' service.

91. **Overseas Bar, World War II** and **Korean War**

These silver bars on navy blue (one for each six months' service) are worn as above, in the same place or above the insigne of rank.

MARINE CORPS INSIGNIA
(ENLISTED MEN)

THE FOLLOWING are the rank insignia of the enlisted men and noncommissioned officers of the United States Marine Corps. These stripes or chevrons are gold on a scarlet background for the dress blue uniform, marine green on red for the green uniform, marine green on khaki for the summer uniform, and even stenciled black on the utility uniform in the field.

92. **Sergeant Major**

This has three chevrons above, four arcs below, and centered between them, a five-pointed star, one point up.

93. **Master Gunnery Sergeant**

This has three chevrons above, four arcs below, and centered between them, a bursting bomb device known as the gunners' emblem.

94. **First Sergeant**

This has three chevrons above, three arcs below, and centered between them, a diamond shape of the same color as the chevrons and arcs.

95. **Master Sergeant**

This has three chevrons above, three arcs below, and centered between them, two crossed 30-caliber service rifles.

96. **Gunnery Sergeant**

This has three chevrons above, two arcs below, and centered between them, two crossed service rifles.

97. **Staff Sergeant**
This has three chevrons above, one arc below, and centered between them, two crossed 30-caliber service rifles.

98. **Sergeant**
This has three chevrons, below which are two crossed 30-caliber service rifles.

99. **Corporal**
This has two chevrons, below which are two crossed 30-caliber service rifles.

100. **Lance Corporal**
This has a single chevron, below which are two crossed 30-caliber service rifles.

101. **Private First Class**
This is a single chevron, point up.

102. **Service Stripes of the Marine Corps**
These are diagonal stripes worn on the lower part of the coat sleeve near the cuff. Each stripe indicates four years' federal service. The three stripes illustrated indicate twelve years' service.

103. **Emblem of the Marine Corps**
This emblem is worn on the hats and lapels of all Marines. The emblem is a globe of the Western Hemisphere. Above this is an American eagle, wings spread and facing left. Behind the globe and diagonally through it is a naval anchor fouled with rope. For enlisted men, the emblem is all bronze; for the dress blue uniform it is all in gold. For officers, the emblem has the eagle and globe in silver, and within the globe the areas of land are in gold; the anchor also is in gold, but the fouled rope is in silver for the dress uniform, all bronze for the service uniform.

The ranks of sergeant major and master gunnery sergeant are new to the Marine Corps.

Originally the chevrons of the Marine Corps were quite large. They were inverted as were the Army's. During World War I, when the smaller style of chevron came into use, and up to World War II, the highest noncommissioned officer rank was

92

93

94

95

96

97

98

99

100

101

102

103

104

105

106

107

108

109

110

111

112

that of first sergeant, and the insignia were the same as those now in use.

Next came first, second, and third grade sergeants, which were separated into both line and staff grades. The arcs, or "rockers," indicated line grade, and straight lines below indicated staff grade. Three arcs indicated first grade, two arcs, second grade, and one arc, third grade.

A musical lyre the same color as the chevron between three chevrons and three arcs indicates the wearer is Marine band leader or second leader of the band. A musical lyre between one chevron and one arc indicates Marine musician.

NAVY AND COAST GUARD INSIGNIA (ENLISTED MEN)

THE FOLLOWING RATINGS, as they are called, are used by both the United States Navy and the United States Coast Guard. They are worn upon the sleeve of the naval jumper, both white and navy blue, and the khaki service coat. When worn on the navy blue uniform, the rank insignia is navy blue and the stripes are red. The eagles and specialty marks are in white. For the white service uniform, they are just the reverse but the stripes are blue. On the khaki uniform they are navy blue or black.

In the illustrations of the petty officers' insignia the specialty marks are those of boatswain. These specialty marks vary, indicating the field a man serves in.

On the blue uniform of petty officers of twelve years or more service with a perfect conduct record the chevrons are in gold. A diagonal stripe worn near the cuff indicates four years of federal service for each stripe — red for the blue uniform, blue for the white, and gold to correspond with the petty officer rating.

104. Chief Master Petty Officer
This has three chevrons, inverted, pointed down. Above them is an arc, and centered in this is an American eagle, wings spread. At the top are two five-pointed stars. Within the arc and chevrons is the specialty mark.

105. Master Petty Officer

This has three chevrons, pointed down, with an arc and the American eagle above. A five-pointed star is centered at the top, and the specialty mark is in the center.

106. Chief Petty Officer

This has three inverted chevrons, point down, with an arc above. Centered on this is an American eagle with wings spread.

107. First Class Petty Officer

This has three inverted chevrons, point down. Above this is an American eagle with wings spread, and the specialty marks are between.

108. Second Class Petty Officer

This has two chevrons inverted and point down. Above this is an American eagle with wings spread. The specialty marks are between.

109. Third Class Petty Officer

This has one inverted chevron, point down. Above this is an American eagle with wings spread. Specialty marks are between.

The above are for naval noncommissioned officers; the following three are for enlisted group rate marks. They are worn between the elbow and the shoulder, and the specialty mark is worn directly above these ratings.

110. Seaman

Three diagonal stripes, one above another.

111. Seaman Apprentice

Two diagonal stripes, one above the other.

112. Seaman Recruit

One diagonal stripe.

NAVY AND COAST GUARD
RATING BADGES AND DISTINGUISHING
OR SPECIALTY MARKS

THE FOLLOWING BADGES are worn by both Navy and Coast Guard personnel. Usually they are worn only as part of the aforementioned rating or rank insignia; however, they are sometimes worn alone. In this case they are known as distinguishing marks rather than specialty marks.

In the beginning, our Navy consisted only of seamen, petty officers, and officers. In the age of sail, a seaman did everything that was ordered, and there were, in effect, no specialists. Of course many of the specialties of today evolved from some sort of special job done by seamen in days past. For instance, the muster roll of the USS *Constellation* in 1798 indicates the presence of a "loblolly boy" aboard ship. Loblolly was a thick gruel, and the boy who served it to the ship's patients became a loblolly boy, for loblolly was also a nautical term for medicine. Later, he came to be called a surgeon's steward, and in 1866 this was changed to apothecary. In 1870 he was called a bayman (probably "sick-bay" man), and by 1898 he had become a hospital steward. Between this time and World War I, he became a hospital apprentice, and in 1917 he became a pharmacist's mate. So the loblolly boy of 1798 eventually became the hospitalman and corpsman of today.

It was not until 1841 that distinguishing marks or specialty marks were prescribed for members of the United States Navy. We shall show these marks in approximately chronological order. Some marks were used first for one specialty and then for another. In that case, we will indicate only the first such use.

113. Boatswain's Mate
This was the first such distinguishing mark adopted. It is two anchors of the period, with long stems and flukes; crossed, and fouled with rope.

114. Master at Arms
A fouled anchor of the period, with a five-pointed star above.

115. Gunner's Mate and **Quarter Gunner**
Two crossed naval cannons, points down.

116. Coxswain
A fouled naval anchor of the period, with flukes down.

117. Quartermaster
A set of early binocular glasses.

118. **Carpenter's Mate**
A naval ax, on an angle, with the head up.

119. **Painter**
A pair of crossed naval axes.

120. **Musician**
A musical lyre.

121. **Ship's Writer**
Two crossed feather pens with points down.

122. **Ship's Cook**
A thick circle with an open center — a doughnut shape.

123. **Sailmaker's Mate**
A marlin spike, used in making sails.

124. **First and Second Captains of Foretop**
A hemp rope in a slipknot.

125. **Captain of Hold**
Two large early keys, crossed, stems down.

126. **Schoolmaster**
An open book.

127. **Ship's Corporal**
A five-pointed star, one point down.

128. **Boatswain's Mate**
This design of two crossed naval anchors is still in use.

129. **Master at Arms**
A five-pointed star with one point up.

130. **Gunner's Mate, Armorer,** and **Quarter Gunner**
Two 12-inch naval rifles, crossed, with muzzles up.

131. **Quartermaster**
A naval steering wheel.

132. **Machinist** and **Boilermaker**
A three-bladed ship's propeller.

133. **Blacksmith**
Two crossed metal hammers.

134. **Coppersmith**
Two sledge hammers crossed.

135. **Sailmaker's Mate**
A half moon with ends to the right.

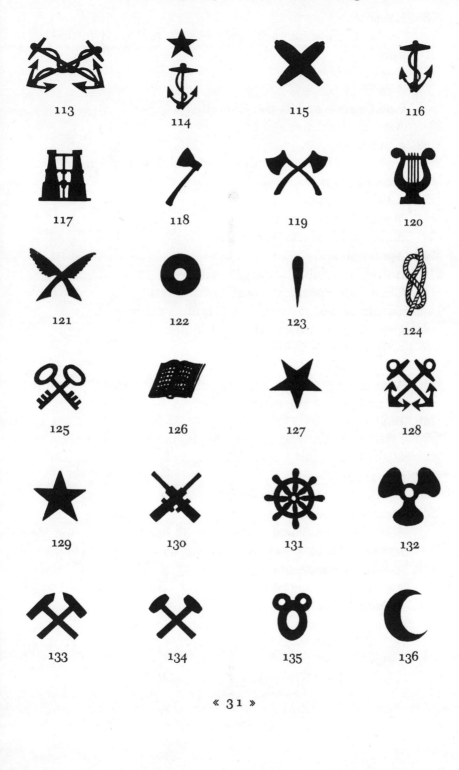

136. **Baker**
A closed clew iron with two eyes, a tool used in making sails.

137. **Bugler**
A military bugle.

138. **Gun Captain** and **Turret Captain**
A naval gun turret and gun.

139. **Electrician**
A globe of the world with latitude and longitude grids.

140. **Seaman Gunner**
A bursting bomb.

141. **Water Tender**
A three-bladed naval propeller.

142. **Apothecary**
A medical symbol, a winged caduceus.

143. **Chief Commissary Steward**
Two interlocking keys, with a quill pen below.

144. **Hospital Steward** and **Hospital Apprentice**
A Geneva cross in red.

145. **Aerographer**
A winged circle with a feathered arrow superimposed on it. Circle is half white and half blue.

146. **Bugler**
Like number 137, a military bugle, but facing the opposite way.

147. **Signalman**
Two square signal flags, crossed.

148. **Motor Machinist's Mate**
A three-bladed naval propeller, with one blade up, and the letters "M" and "O" at either side of the top blade.

149. **Aviation Ordnanceman**
A winged bursting bomb.

150. **Aviation Pilot**
A naval anchor, with a shield superimposed and wings attached.

151. **Aviation Machinist's Mate**
A single-bladed winged airplane propeller.

137

138

139

140

141

142

143

144

145

146

147

148

149

150

151

152

153

154

155

156

157

152. **Radioman**
A series of lightning bolts or electrical sparks.

153. **Torpedoman**
A naval torpedo with fins, facing right.

154. **Aviation Metalsmith**
A pair of crossed metal sledge hammers, with wings.

155. **Aviation Rigger**
A winged rigging loop or rigging device.

156. **Aviation Carpenter's Mate**
Two crossed wood axes, with wings.

157. **Photographer**
A large, early-style camera.

158. **Airship Rigger**
A naval anchor with flukes down. Superimposed on this is a lighter-than-air dirigible. This design is winged.

159. **Fire Controlman**
A naval range-finding device mounted on a tripod.

160. **Aviation Electrician's Mate**
A winged globe of the world.

161. **Parachute Rigger**
The open canopy and shroud lines of a winged parachute.

162. **Aviation Radioman** and **Aviation Radio Technician**
The sparks or lightning bolts of the radioman's device, winged.

163. **Gunner's Mate**
Two naval rifles (cannons), crossed barrels up.

164. **Boatswain's Mate** and **Coxswain**
Two naval anchors, crossed and with flukes down.

165. **Mineman**
A naval floating mine, with wavy lines, representing the sea, under it.

166. **Radarman**
Three sparks or lightning bolts with an arrow diagonally through them. The point of the arrow is uppermost.

167. **Special Artificer**
An engineer's caliper, slightly open and with points down.

168. Sonarman and **Soundman**

A headset of earphones, open at the bottom, with an Indian arrow, pointed left, through it.

169. Ship's Service Man

A key, teeth down, and a feather or quill pen, point down, crossed diagonally.

170. Torpedoman's Mate

A new-style naval torpedo, much slimmer than the one previously used, and without the fin guard.

171. Yeoman

Two crossed quill pens, points down.

The following badges were worn only during World War II, and they were known as Navy specialist ratings. They were also worn by the Coast Guard. They were all similar in design (a diamond outline or frame, with a gothic letter or letters centered within it). We show only one but we describe all the others.

[172.] Navy Specialist Ratings

The letter "A" for physical training instructor (172); "C" for classification interviewer; "F" for fire fighter; "G" for aviation free gunnery instructor; "I" for accounting or punch-card machine operator; "M" for mail; "O" for inspector of naval matériel; "P" for photograph specialist; "Q" for communication specialist; "R" for recruiter; "S" for shore patrol; "T" for teacher; "V" for transport airman; "W" for chaplain's assistant; "X" for specialist not classified elsewhere; "Y" for control operator or control tower man; "D" for dog patrol; "CB" for construction battalions, Seabees. The following were worn only in the Coast Guard: "PS" for port security; "TR" for transport; and "CW" for chemical warfare.

173. Aviation, General Utility

A small winged washer or circle.

174. Navy "E"

Worn by all enlisted naval personnel of ships, carriers, or squadrons awarded a battle efficiency pennant. Subsequent awards are indicated by a diagonal stripe or stripes placed under the "E."

175. **Bombsight Mechanic**
The letter "B" in gothic form, centered, with triangles on either side.

176. **Air Gunner**
An airplane's 50-caliber machine gun, winged, at an angle.

177. **Gun Captain**
A large naval rifle or cannon with axis horizontal and muzzle to the right.

178. **Ordnance Battalion**
The letters "OB" in gothic form.

179. **Mine Warfare**
A circle (representing a mine) atop a square (representing an anchor). It portrays an anchored mine.

180. **Submarine Insigne**
This is the same design carried out in the silver and gold badges outlined in the section on qualification badges (p. 88). It has waves at the bottom with a submarine running on the surface, and at either side are dolphins.

181. **Gun Pointer Second Class** and **Gun Director Pointer**
A gun sight with cross wires and square center section. For the Gun Pointer First Class, it is the same device, with a five-pointed star, point up, above.

182. **Rifle Sharpshooter**
A square rifle target with ring and bull's-eye. The Expert insigne has a second inner ring, the Marksman only a bull's-eye.

183. **Horizontal Bomber**
A sighting device or sight with an aerial bomb centered within. The Master Horizontal Bomber insigne has a five-pointed star above.

184. **Air Defense Gunner**
A gun sight with an airplane centered in it.

185. **Airship Insigne**
The badge shows a lighter-than-air dirigible and is worn by all personnel assigned to these craft.

186. **Deep-Sea Diver**
This shows a diving helmet and breastplate. Within the

158

159

160

161

162

163

164

165

166

167

168

169

170

171

172

173

174

175

176

177

178

179

180

181

182

183

184

185

186

187

188

189

190

191

192

193

194

195

196

197

198

199

200

201

202

203

204

breastplate, the numeral "1" means first class diver; "2" means second class diver; the letter "S" means salvage diver; and the letters "SD" mean scuba diver.

187. **Master Deep-Sea Diver**
This is the same design as above, but with the letter "M" in the breastplate.

188. **Radar Fire Controlman**
This shows a range-finding device on a tripod with a radar screen, showing a horizontal zigzag line, superimposed on it.

189. **Postal Clerk**
A postmark such as is made by a postage meter.

190. **Aviation Boatswain's Mate**
Crossed anchors, flukes down, and winged.

191. **Aviation Fire Control Technician**
A naval range-finder on a tripod and winged.

192. **Expert Lookout**
A pair of naval binoculars, objective lens down.

193. **Air Crewman**
A winged circle with the letters "AC," for air crew.

194. **Fire Fighter Assistant**
A Maltese cross.

195. **Radarman**
An A-scope is superimposed on a diagonal arrow, point up.

196. **Quartermaster**
A ship's wheel or helm.

197. **Missile Technician**
A guided missile surrounded by an electronic wave in an oval shape.

198. **Nuclear Weapons Man**
An atomic bomb with the device of a helium atom around it.

199. **Electronics Technician**
This helium atom device has two ovals with stars and dots.

200. **Optical Man**
Double concave and convex lenses, with two lines passing through them.

201. **Teleman**
A postal mark, as is used for the Postal Clerk Badge. Super-

imposed on this are a lightning bolt and quill pen, points down and crossed.

202. Communications Technician

A quill pen crossed by a lightning bolt or spark.

203. Personnel Man

A large book, spine left, and behind it a feather or quill pen, point down.

204. Machine Accountant

A quill pen superimposed diagonally on a gear wheel.

205. Assault Boat Coxswain

Crossed plain anchors, with a superimposed arrowhead pointing toward the front. The arrowhead resembles a rocket.

206. Explosive Ordnance Disposal Technician

A sea mine, with a crossed torpedo and an aircraft bomb superimposed. Both explosives are point down.

207. Disbursing Clerk

A check or IBM card, with a key superimposed thereon.

208. Journalist

A scroll, with a quill pen crossed diagonally at its front.

209. Lithographer

A lithograph crayon holder and lithograph scraper, crossed and points up.

210. Illustrator Draftsman

A triangle with a draftsman's compass superimposed on it.

211. Engineman

A small circular device within a wide gear wheel or cog-wheel.

212. Machinery Repairman

A micrometer; within the open end is a gear wheel.

213. Boilerman

A Hero's boiler with discharge vents emitting steam puffs.

214. Boilermaker

The same device as the above (213), with a two-headed wrench of the sort used by mechanics superimposed diagonally across it.

205

206

207

208

209

210

211

212

213

214

215

216

217

218

219

220

221

222

223

224

225

226

227

228

215. **Interior Communications Electrician**

A globe of the world, of the type used by electricians. Above this is a French-type phone as used aboard ships.

216. **Pipe Fitter**

Two crossed monkey wrenches, as used in plumbing or pipe-fitting work.

217. **Damage Controlman**

A fire-fighting ax and a sledge hammer, crossed.

218. **Patternmaker**

A wooden jack plane facing toward the front.

219. **Molder**

A bench rammer and a stove tool, crossed.

220. **Engineering Aide**

A leveling rod, with a measuring scale toward the front.

221. **Construction Electrician**

A spark or lightning bolt superimposed upon a telephone pole.

222. **Equipment Operator**

A bulldozer, blade toward the front.

223. **Construction Mechanic**

A double-headed wrench superimposed upon a large nut.

224. **Builder**

A carpenter's square, point up, superimposed on a plumb bob.

225. **Steel Worker**

A large I beam suspended from a derrick hook.

226. **Utilities Man**

A pipe valve, with the connection to the left and the wheel on top.

227. **Aviation Machinist's Mate**

A single-blade propeller with wings at either side.

228. **Steward**

An open book; upon it, a key and a wheat spike, crossed.

229. **Aviation Electronics Technician**

A helium atom device with two winged electrons.

230. **Aviation Guided Missileman**

A missile within a winged oval electrical border.

231. **Air Controlman**
   A winged microphone.
232. **Aviation Anti-Submarine Warfare Technician**
   A lightning bolt above and pointing down toward waves (representing the sea). Below the waves is an arrow pointing down. This design is winged.
233. **Aviation Maintenance Administration**
   An open book, with a double-bladed airplane propeller toward the front of the badge and wings to either side of the book.
234. **Aviation Storekeeper**
   Crossed keys, winged.
235. **Photographic Intelligenceman**
   A stereoscope and a graphic solution of a photographic problem (somewhat resembling a winged symbol).
236. **Photographer's Mate**
   A graphic solution of a photographic problem, with lenses in the center.
237. **Tradesman**
   A spark or lightning bolt passing diagonally through a gear wheel.
238. **Data Systems Technician**
   A helium atom design with three surrounding arrows pointing toward its center and one pointing out from the center.
239. **Aviation Ordnanceman**
   A bursting bomb, winged.
240. **Hospital Corpsman**
   A caduceus.
241. **Dental Technician**
   A caduceus with a gothic "D" superimposed.
242. **Chief Petty Officer Hat Emblem**
   A naval anchor, flukes down and fouled with a rope, all in gold. In front are the letters "U.S.N." in silver in a circular form.
243. **Coast Guard Shield**
   A shield worn on the lower uniform sleeve. There are stripes in the lower area and stars in the chief, or upper part, of the

229

230

231

232

233

234

235

236

237

238

239

240

241

242

243

244

245

246

shield. For officers it is in gold, for chief petty officers it is in silver, and for enlisted men it is in blue or white, according to the uniform.

244. Naval Reserve Merchant Marine Emblem

This emblem in gold is worn on the left breast of the uniform coat by members of the Merchant Marine holding commands in the Naval Reserve. It is an American eagle with wings spread, and an American shield on its breast. A wide scroll pattern below bears the letters "USNR" (for United States Naval Reserve).

245. Coast Guard Officer Hat Emblem

An American eagle, wings spread, in gold. In front of it is the shield of the Coast Guard in silver. Below it is a wide anchor with its flukes facing to the right. The anchor is fouled with rope and it is all in silver.

246. Chief Petty Officer Emblem

Worn on the hat and collar. It is an anchor, flukes down, fouled with rope. The entire design is carried out in gold. Superimposed upon the anchor is the shield of the Coast Guard, in silver.

NAVY CORPS DEVICES

THE FOLLOWING DEVICES in gold are embroidered upon the uniform or worn as metal devices on the collar in gold.

247. Line Officer

A five-pointed star, one point down.

248. Medical Corps

A spread oak leaf with a silver acorn in the center.

249. Dental Corps

A spread oak leaf with acorns at either side of the stem.

250. Supply Corps

A sprig of three oak leaves with three acorns.

251. Christian Chaplain

A Latin cross worn at an angle.

252. Jewish Chaplain

A star of David atop the Hebrew tablets of the law.

253. **Hospital Corps**
Wings and a caduceus. The snakes of the caduceus have red tongues.

254. **Civil Engineering Corps**
Two sprigs of two oak leaves and two acorns. The acorns are in silver.

255. **Women Accepted for Volunteer Emergency Service (WAVES) — World War II**
A naval anchor, fouled with rope, all in silver. Behind it is a three-bladed naval propeller in blue metal.

256. **Midshipman — U.S. Naval Academy**
The collar device is shown. It is a rather long naval anchor, in gold, on its side. The cap insigne is similar, except that the anchor is fouled with rope and is worn with the flukes down.

257. **Navy Nurse Corps**
A spread oak leaf, in gold, with an acorn centered in it. Within the leaf are the letters "NNC," for Navy Nurse Corps, in silver.

All the following devices, for chief warrant officers, are in silver and are worn in the same manner as the above.

258. **Chief Boatswain** and **Boatswain**
Crossed naval anchors fouled with rope.

259. **Chief Carpenter** and **Carpenter**
A carpenter's square, point down.

260. **Chief Electrician** and **Electrician**
A globe showing lines of latitude and longitude.

261. **Chief Photographer** and **Photographer**
An old-style folding type camera.

262. **Chief Gunner** and **Gunner**
A bursting bomb device.

263. **Chief Machinist** and **Machinist**
A three-bladed ship's propeller, one blade up.

264. **Chief Pharmacist** and **Pharmacist**
A caduceus, in silver.

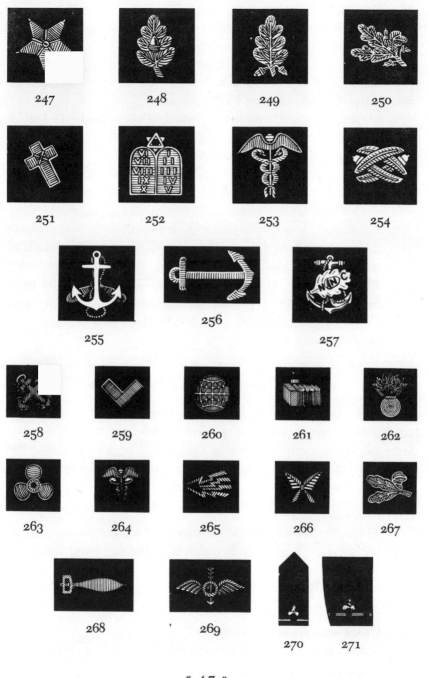

247

248

249

250

251

252

253

254

255

256

257

258

259

260

261

262

263

264

265

266

267

268

269

270

271

265. Chief Radio Electrician and **Radio Electrician**
Four bolts of lightning or sparks.

266. Chief Ship's Clerk and **Ship's Clerk**
Two crossed quill pens, points down.

267. Chief Pay Clerk and **Pay Clerk**
A sprig of three oak leaves.

268. Chief Torpedoman and **Torpedoman**
A naval torpedo, with fin guard. The torpedo is facing right.

269-271. Chief Aerographer and **Aerographer**
A circle divided in halves by the shaft of an arrow. The arrowhead points down and the feathers point up. The center circle design is winged.

These devices for pinning on the collar of the uniform shirt are in silver (269). They are in silver bullion cloth to attach to the shoulder board (270), or above the warrant officer stripe or sleeve stripe (271). The illustrations used for the rank insignia at the beginning of this section showed all the warrant officers' ranks with the crossed anchors of the boatswain rating.

ARMY CORPS INSIGNIA

THE FOLLOWING CLOTH INSIGNIA were first used in the 1880s and continued in use through the period of World War I. When the large chevrons were used, these insignia were placed above the chevrons, which at that time were reversed. The first illustration indicates how they were used with the chevrons of World War I.

272. Color Sergeant
Three stripes or chevrons above and an arc design below; within them is an open five-pointed star, one point up.

These insignia were also worn on the sleeve, within the chevron. If no chevron was authorized, they were worn near the cuff.

273. Gun Pointer, Coast Artillery
A red circle on a blue disk. Within the blue field are crossed

field artillery pieces, also in red. A small bar below the guns would indicate gun commander.

274. Engineer, Coast Artillery

A red circle on a blue disk. Within the blue field is an engine governor.

275. Second Class Observer, Coast Artillery

A blue disk with a circle of red near the edge. Within this is a triangle of red. A bar below the triangle would indicate first class gunner and plotter.

276. Chief Planter and Chief Loader, Coast Artillery

A blue disk with a circle of red near the edge. In the center is a mine case, with an anchoring device below. A bar below this, between the mine and the circle, would indicate casemate electrician.

277. Excellence in Target Practice Badge, Coast Artillery

A blue disk with the numeral "1," centered, in red.

278. Second Class Gunner, Coast Artillery

A blue disk with a red projectile, point up and centered. A bar below the shell would indicate first class gunner.

279. Farrier, Cavalry

A blue disk bearing a horse's head in yellow.

280. Hospital Man, Medical Corps

A blue disk with a caduceus in maroon piped in white at the center.

281. Signal Corps Insigne

A blue disk with the design of the Signal Corps (crossed signal flags) on an upright signal torch.

282. Cook's Insigne

A blue disk, with a white cook's hat in the center. It is sometimes called a "loaf of bread" because of its shape.

283. Engineer Corps Insigne

A blue disk with the castle insigne of the Engineer Corps in scarlet piped in white at the center.

284. Saddler, Cavalry

A blue disk with a saddler's round knife, edge up, in yellow.

285. Drummer's Insigne

A blue disk with crossed drum sticks in white at the center.

272

273

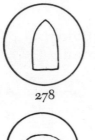

274

275

276

277

278

279

280

281

282

283

284

285

286

287

288

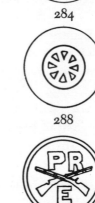

289

290

291

292

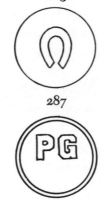

293

286. Mechanic and **Artificer**

A blue disk with crossed sledges or mallets in white at the center.

287. Horseshoer, Cavalry

A blue disk with a horseshoe, toe up, in yellow.

288. Wagoner, Cavalry or **Infantry**

A blue disk with an eight-spoke wheel at the center. The wheel is in white for the infantry and yellow for the cavalry.

All the preceding disks, which had a blue background, were used when the uniform was blue. They were changed to army brown when a uniform of that color was adopted in 1916.

With the advent of new systems and the new field uniform in the Army during World War I, a new type of collar ornament was prescribed. This was the circular disk worn on the high-standing collar of the service coat. Officers, however, continued to wear these devices without a circular disk. All the new devices were in dark bronze.

A number of the disks, which were used for a very short period, are shown. Other disks, which came into use during this period and are in use to the present day, follow.

289. Electrician

A device of five forked lightning bolts, joined to an oval at the bottom, within a circular outer ring.

290. Infantry Collar Disk

Two crossed muskets, the infantry insignia, above which appears the regimental number (in this case, the Thirtieth) and below, the company (in this case, "M" Company). For the artillery, crossed cannon replaced the muskets; for the cavalry, crossed sabers in sheaths. It is all in bronze.

291. Prison Guard

The usual bronze disk, with the letters "PG" slightly above center.

292. Infantry, Puerto Rico Regiment

The usual bronze disk, with the center design indicating the branch of service (in this case, infantry). The letters

"PR" stand for Puerto Rico, and the company letter is below.

293. Infantry, Philippines — Native Troops

The usual bronze disk. The center design indicates the branch of service (in this case, infantry). The letter "P" stands for Philippines. The numeral below indicates the native infantry regiment number.

294. Recruiting Service

The usual bronze disk. The letters "RS" stand for Recruiting Service, and the numeral below is the recruiting district (in this case, the twelfth).

295. Quartermaster Corps

The usual bronze disk. The emblem of the Quartermaster Corps, a wheel with spokes, is at the center and on the outer rim are thirteen stars. In front of the wheel are a key and an Army sword, crossed, and above it is an American eagle.

The following five insignia, shown here as officers' emblems, were used in World Wars I and II. The insignia were within a disk and carried out in dark bronze for World War I; in World War II they were carried out in bright brass or gold color.

The following section lists the badges currently in use in the United States Army.

296. Army Air Corps

A double-bladed airplane propeller in silver. The wings are in gold.

297. Armored Center and Units

A Mark VIII tank, used in World War I, in gold.

298. Cavalry

Two crossed cavalry sabers, cased.

299. Field Artillery

Two light field guns of the Civil War period, crossed, in gold.

300. Coast Artillery

Two coastal cannons of the Civil War period, crossed, in

gold. Centered in them is a gold oval with a red enameled center, and a gold artillery shell centered on that.

301. **Medical Administrative Corps**
This and the following four insignia have a central design, which is the caduceus, the symbol of the Medical Corps. The letters used are dark brown, almost black, in appearance and signify the wearer's specialty. This insigne bears the caduceus with the letter "A," for Administrative.

302. **Physical Therapy Aide**
The caduceus with the letters "PT," for physical therapy.

303. **Contract Surgeon**
The caduceus with the letter "C" at the center.

304. **Hospital Dietitian**
The caduceus with the letters "HD" at the center.

305. **Pharmacy Corps**
The caduceus with the letter "P" centered.

306. **Military Intelligence Reserve**
A sculptured shield with "ears." The Sphinx is pictured at the center.

307. **Tank Destroyer Units**
A tracked vehicle, the M-3, carrying a 75-mm antitank gun.

308. **Woman's Army Corps (WAC)**
The head of Pallas Athene, the Greek goddess of war, in a Greek war helmet, facing left.

309. **Army Band**
A large musical Lyre, with the letters "U.S." superimposed.

310. **First Special Service Force**
Two crossed Indian arrows. This was the insigne of the Indian scouts, who, many years ago, were the predecessors of the Rangers and the Special Forces.

311. **Bomb Disposal Personnel**
This was a patch worn on the uniform sleeve. It is black, round at the top and pointed at the bottom. Within it is an aerial bomb in scarlet, outlined in gold.

312. **Coast Artillery Corps Excellence Insigne**
A disk of army brown, with a gothic letter "E" in scarlet. It is of cloth and was worn on the uniform coat sleeve.

-94

295

296

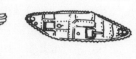

297

298

299

300

301

302

303

304

305

306

307

308

309

310

311

312

There are references to a Tank-Infantry insigne, which bore the crossed rifles or muskets of the infantry, and a very early-style tank, as used in World War I, centered on it. But there is no official reference to it, and it is not illustrated here.

The following insignia of branch of service are in use at present in the United States Army.

313, 314. Adjutant General's Corps

For officers the insigne is a shield with a chief of blue and one large and twelve small stars in white, on the blue (313). The lower half has seven white and six red vertical stripes. For enlisted men the same shield is on a disk, and both are in gold (314).

315. Armor Corps

An M-26 tank, with raised gun superimposed on two crossed cavalry sabers in scabbards. It is in gold color for officers. The design is the same for enlisted men, but it is all within a disk.

316. Artillery

A missile surmounting two crossed field guns, all in gold, for officers. The design is the same for enlisted men, but it is all within a disk.

317. Army Medical Corps

A caduceus in gold color.

318. Dental Corps

A caduceus in gold color. The letter "D" superimposed is in black.

319. Medical Service Corps

A caduceus in gold with the letters "MS" in a monogram in black.

320. Veterinary Corps

A caduceus in gold, with the letter "V" superimposed in black.

321. Army Medical Specialist Corps

A caduceus in gold, with the letter "S" superimposed in black.

313

314

315

316

317

318

319

320

321

322

323

324

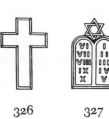

325

326

327

328

329

330

331

332

333

334

335

336

337

322. Army Nurse Corps

A caduceus in gold, with the letter "N" in black.

323. Army Medical Corps Enlisted Personnel

A caduceus of gold color within a disk.

324. Unassigned to Branch, Enlisted Personnel

The Coat of Arms of the United States on a disk.

325. Intelligence and Security Branch

On a golden dagger, point up, is a gold heraldic sunburst of four straight and four wavy points. In front of this is a gold heraldic rose with petals of dark blue, edged in gold. The design for enlisted men is the same but within a disk and all in gold.

326. Christian Chaplain

A Latin cross in silver.

327. Jewish Chaplain

The double tablet of Jewish laws (the Ten Commandments) with a star of David atop the tablets. It is all in silver.

328. Chemical Corps

A benzene ring of cobalt blue superimposed at the center of two crossed retorts (test tubes). For enlisted men the design is the same but on a disk all in gold.

329. Army General Staff

This design bears the Coat of Arms of the United States in gold. The shield is in color. The whole is superimposed upon a five-pointed star of silver with one point up. For enlisted personnel the design is in a disk and all in gold color.

330. Civil Affairs, USAR

On an armillary globe is a stylized torch of Liberty surmounted by a rolled scroll, and a sword, which are crossed in saltier. The design is in gold. The enlisted men's insigne is the same within a disk.

331. Corps of Engineers

A triple-turreted castle in gold. For enlisted men the design is the same, within a disk, and all gold.

332. Finance Corps

A lined gold-colored diamond. For enlisted men the design is the same in a disk.

333. Infantry

For officers, two early military muskets, crossed in gold. For enlisted men the same design is within a disk, and all in gold.

334. Inspector General's Staff

A sword and fasces crossed and wreathed in gold. In front of this is a wreath with the motto *"Droit et Avant"* ("Right and Forward") in green or blue enamel in the upper part of the wreath.

335. Judge Advocate General's Corps

A gold-colored sword and quill pen crossed and to the front of an open wreath of laurel leaves knotted at the bottom. This is in gold.

336. Military Police Corps

Two early flintlock pistols, crossed, in gold, for officers. The design is the same for enlisted men, but is within a disk of gold.

337. National Guard Bureau

Two crossed fasces, in gold, superimposed on an American eagle with its wings reversed. The same design for enlisted men is within a disk and in gold.

338. Ordnance Corps

An early-style grenade, or bursting bomb, in gold color. The design is the same for enlisted men, except that it is within a gold disk.

339. Quartermaster Corps

For officers, a gold-colored sword and key, crossed, on a wheel surmounted by a flying eagle in gold. The background is a wheel of blue, and its hub center is red. Edged in white on the blue wheel rim are thirteen white stars. The same insigne on a disk, all in gold, is for enlisted men.

340. Signal Corps

For officers, two signal flags, crossed. The one at the left is white with a red center square, and the one on the right is red with a white center. Both are edged in gold. A flaming torch of gold color is upright in the center. The same design all in gold within a disk is for enlisted men.

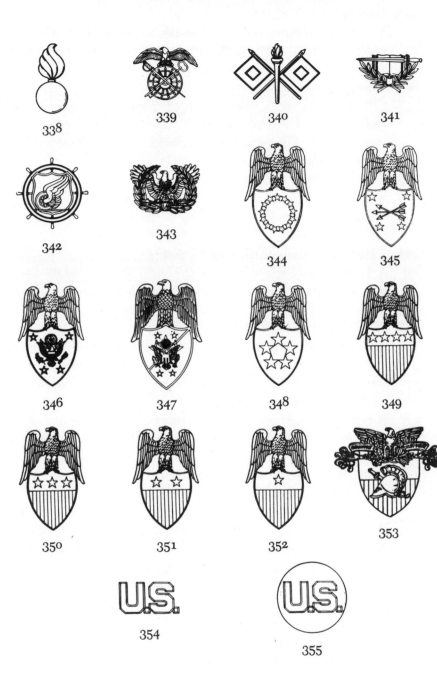

338

339

340

341

342

343

344

345

346

347

348

349

350

351

352

353

354

355

341. **Staff Specialist, USAR**
A sword laid horizontally across the upper part of an open book. Below the book and around it are two laurel branches, which are crossed at the stems. All this is in gold color.

342. **Transportation Corps**
For officers, a ship's steering wheel. Superimposed on it is a shield charged with a winged car wheel on a rail. All this is in gold color. The same design is used for enlisted personnel but is enclosed within a disk.

343. **Warrant Officer Emblem**
An American eagle with wings spread standing on two arrows. This design is enclosed by a wreath of laurel leaves and is all in gold.

344. **Aide to President of the United States**
A blue-colored shield with a circle of thirteen white five-pointed stars in the center. The shield is surmounted by a gold-colored eagle, with its wings reversed.

345. **Aide to Secretary of Defense**
A blue shield with three crossed arrows in gold and four five-pointed enameled stars in white. A gold eagle is atop the shield.

346. **Aide to Secretary of the Army**
A red shield with the Coat of Arms of the United States in gold, centered, and four white enameled stars near the corner. A gold eagle is atop the shield. The same design on a white shield is for Aide to Under Secretary of the Army.

347. **Aide to Chief of Staff**
A shield divided diagonally with the upper part in red and the lower part in white. At the center is a silver five-pointed star. Superimposed upon this is the Coat of Arms of the United States in full color; above it are two white stars and below it, two red ones. Atop the shield is an American eagle in gold.

348. **Aide to General of the Army**
A blue shield with five white stars arranged in a circle, their inner points touching. Atop the shield is an American eagle with wings reversed and all in gold.

349. Aide to General

A shield with a blue chief. Below this are seven white and six red vertical stripes. In the blue chief are four white five-pointed stars. The whole is surmounted by an American eagle in gold. The same pattern is used for the following three insignia (350–52); only the number of stars changes. The stars correspond to the rank of the general whose aide the wearer is. The stars all are white enamel.

350. Aide to Lieutenant General

The same insigne as that of general's aide, but with three white stars in the blue chief within the shield.

351. Aide to Major General

The same insigne as that of general's aide, but with two white stars in the blue chief of the shield.

352. Aide to Brigadier General

The same insigne as that of general's aide, but with one white star in the blue chief of the shield.

353. United States Military Academy

This insigne is worn by permanent professors, registrars, and civilian instructors at the Academy. It is the Coat of Arms of the Military Academy: the shield of the United States, bearing the helmet of Pallas over a Greek sword and surmounted by an eagle, displayed with a scroll and the motto "Duty, Honor, Country West Point MDCCCV USMA" all in gold.

354. Officers' Insigne

The gothic letters "U.S." in gold. It is both lapel and collar insigne for commissioned officers of the Army.

355. Enlisted Mens' Collar Insigne

The gothic letters "U.S." on a circular disk, all in gold. It is worn on the left lapel of the uniform shirt and coat.

PART II

Qualification Badges

1

2

3

4

5   6

7   8

9   10

THESE BADGES, awarded for highly specialized qualification in certain military fields and for service that is not considered within the usual requirements of these fields, are worn by such members of the military as submarine and flight personnel, airborne paratroopers, and deep-sea divers. The men and women who wear them usually receive extra pay for their specialties. Qualification badges for proficiency with certain military weapons are commonly called shooting badges, and are dealt with in a separate section.

Aviation qualification devices, commonly known as wings, are prescribed by the military services for wear on uniforms to indicate qualification in aviation and are designated as "aviation badges." Badges indicate qualification in certain fields. These are worn on the left breast, above the line of decorations, medals, or service ribbons, with the exception of the original Military Aviator Badge and certain other insignia, which are worn below the service ribbons.

The badges of the Army and the Air Force are in silver, with the exception of the Military Aviator Badge, the earlier cloth flight badges (1917–18), and the original Flight Surgeon and Flight Nurse badges, which are in gold. The aviation badges of the Navy, Marine Corps, and Coast Guard are in gold, with the exception of the original Air Crew Badge, in silver, and the enlisted rating badges, which are in woven cloth.

America's first military aviation badges were awarded more than fifty years ago, in the fall of 1913. One of the first twelve pilots to be awarded the "golden eagle" badge of military aviator was Lieutenant Henry H. ("Hap") Arnold. He later pencil-sketched the design for the wings awarded during World War I. Still, later, during World War II, this same Hap Arnold, wearing the five stars of the highest general officer as Commanding General, USAAF, painted this word picture of what these badges stand for when he said, "Silver wings are the badge of combat and devotion to duty. They represent the pilots . . . the bombardiers . . . the navigators . . . the gunners . . . the mechanics . . . the officers . . . the enlisted men. Silver wings are a symbol of America . . . our country . . . our flag . . . the love that all of us feel for our free and proud homeland."

One of the requirements for earning the Military Aviator Badge in 1913 was that the aspiring aeronaut "attain an altitude of at least 2500 feet as recorded on a barograph." To qualify as a pilot astronaut today, he must be qualified to pilot powered vehicles that are capable of flights above 50 miles, or 264,000 feet, and the astronaut must have made at least one such flight.

Regulation-size badges are 3⅛ inches wide, and miniatures are 2 inches wide.

ARMY BADGES

1. **Military Aviator Badge (Original)**

   This was the first military badge awarded for qualification in the air, authorized on May 27, 1913, and awarded to fourteen officers then on duty with the Signal Corps. Those fourteen badges were struck in gold, and the fact that early aviators were in the Signal Corps of the United States Army is indicated by the design. The decorative top bar has the words "military aviator" in capital letters. Below it, suspended by links, is a strikingly detailed eagle, with wings outspread. Its talons grasp the flags used in the insigne of the Signal Corps.

2. **Military Aviator (1917)**

   This badge is embroidered on dark blue felt. The wings and the shield of the United States are in silver bullion, and the "U.S." is in gold bullion. The wings are regulation size, 3 inches.

3. Junior Military Aviator (1917)

This badge is embroidered on dark blue felt, and is almost an exact duplicate of the Military Aviator, except that it has but one wing. It is often referred to as a "half wing." The shield and wing are in silver bullion, and the "U.S." in in gold. The size of the wing is about 2 inches.

4. Enlisted Pilot (1917)

This badge is embroidered on dark blue felt. In the center is a four-bladed propeller, and on either side are half wings embroidered in white silk. These wings were worn on the sleeve.

5. Aviation Mechanic (1917)

This badge is embroidered on dark blue felt. The design consists of a rather large four-bladed propeller within a white embroidered circle. Above this often appears a numeral, which is the designation of the unit to which the mechanic was assigned. This patch was worn on the sleeve.

6. Other Aviation Ratings

This badge is embroidered, and is the same as the Aviation Mechanic Badge (5), but without the outer circle. It was worn on the sleeve.

7. Military Aviator (Third Style)

This embroidered badge was approved on October 27, 1917. It is of silver bullion on dark blue felt, with the "U.S." in gold. The design is exactly the same as the second style Military Aviator Badge (2), with the addition of a silver bullion five-pointed star centered directly above the shield in the center.

8. Junior and Reserve Military Aviator

This badge is embroidered, and is exactly the same as the second style Military Aviator Badge (2). It was also approved October 27, 1917.

9. Observer Badge

This embroidered badge is exactly the same as the original Junior Military Aviator Badge (3). It was also approved on October 27, 1917.

10. **Observer Badge (Second Style)**

This embroidered badge is silver bullion on dark blue cloth. It is a "half wing," like the previous Observer Badge (9), but in place of the shield, there appears a letter "O." It was authorized for wear on December 29, 1917.

11. **Military Aeronaut**

This badge, embroidered in white silk on dark blue felt, was worn by pilots of the Lighter-than-Air Service and Balloon Corps. In the center of the wings is a balloon and suspending basket, and in the center of the balloon are the letters "U.S." in gold. Centered above the basket is a five-pointed star in white silk. It was authorized on December 29, 1917.

12. **Junior** and **Reserve Military Aeronaut**

This badge is embroidered in white silk on dark blue felt. These wings are identical to the Military Aeronaut Badge (11), except that they have no five-pointed star above. The "U.S." is in gold.

13. **Military Aviator (Fourth Style)** and **Junior** and **Reserve Military Aviator**

Authorized on December 21, 1918, this and the following two badges were the first oxidized silver badges authorized. The Military Aviator Badge is regulation size, 3⅛ inches. The design is the same as the third style Military Aviator Badge. It has straight silver wings, in the center of which is a shield of the United States in oxidized silver, on which the letters "U.S." are in gold. It is a pin-back badge, to be worn on the left breast over the pocket.

14. **Military Aeronaut** and **Junior** and **Reserve Military Aeronaut**

This badge, authorized on December 21, 1918, is oxidized silver. It consists of straight silver wings. Centered in the wings is a balloon with a suspending basket. The letters "U.S." in gold are centered on the balloon.

15. **Observer (Third Style)**

This badge, in oxidized silver, is a "half wing" to the right of an "O" shape around the letters "U.S." in gold.

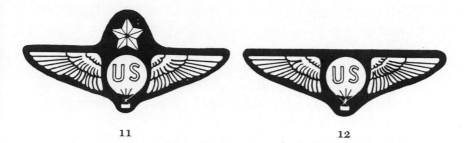

11   12

13

14   15

16   17

18   19

16. **Military Aviator** and **Junior** and **Reserve Military Aviator** (**Fifth Style**)

This badge was authorized on January 25, 1919. It set a new pattern for wings and is still in use. The wings, made of oxidized silver, are a bit more decorative than previous styles. They are nicely sculptured, and the ends sweep up. This type of wings will be referred to as "usual style" hereafter. The two spread wings bear an American shield in the center.

17. **Military Aeronaut** and **Junior** and **Reserve Military Aeronaut** (**Third Style**)

This badge, authorized on January 25, 1919, for qualified balloon pilots, is in oxidized silver. It has two spread wings, usual style, with a balloon and suspending basket in the center. It is interesting to note that the balloon was the type in use at the time of introduction of the badge, while the previous badge showed the earlier-style balloon — an example of insignia showing the advances of warfare and science.

18. **Observer** (**Fourth Style**)

This badge was authorized on January 25, 1919, for qualified military air observers. It is a half wing, of the new sculptured style. To the left of the wing is a circle and within the circle are the letters "U.S." It is all in oxidized silver.

19. **Pilot Observer**

This badge was authorized on November 12, 1920. The spread wings bear a circle with the letters "U.S." in the center. It is the usual style and standard size in oxidized silver. This badge was worn by military observers who were qualified as pilots.

20. **Airplane Pilot**

This badge was authorized on October 14, 1921. It is made of oxidized silver and is the same as the previously adopted Military Aviator Badge (16), fifth style. Only the designation has changed. It was authorized for all qualified airplane pilots of the Army Air Force.

21. **Airship Pilot**

This badge was authorized on October 14, 1921, for quali-

20

21

22

23

24

25

26

27

28

fied pilots of the Lighter-than-Air Service and for military aeronauts. It is in oxidized silver and has the usual style of wings with a dirigible centered on them.

22. Airplane Observer

This badge was authorized on October 14, 1921, for observers in military aircraft who were not qualified as pilots. It is the same style and design as the previously authorized pilot observer wings except that the "U.S." has been removed. The airplane pilot wings would take precedence over these wings.

23. Balloon Observer

This badge was authorized on October 14, 1921. It is the same badge as that of the military aeronaut or balloon pilot authorized on January 25, 1919. The badge is oxidized silver.

Embroidered Badges Authorized

These were authorized for wear on October 14, 1921. Parallel with the four styles just mentioned were the same style of badges embroidered in white silk for wear on the wool service coat only.

24. Pilot Badge

This badge, authorized on November 10, 1941, is the same as that of the airplane pilot; only the designation has changed. It is made of oxidized silver.

25. Senior Pilot Badge

This badge was authorized on November 10, 1941, for pilots with a specified number of hours in the air and years of service. With the growth of the AAF, it was decided that senior airmen should have a distinctive badge to show the difference in flying time and time in grade. At the same time, pilots would have higher qualifications to strike for. The badge, in oxidized silver, is the same as the Pilot's Badge, with the addition of a silver five-pointed star, one point up, centered directly above the shield.

26. Command Pilot Badge

This badge, authorized on November 10, 1941, is for senior pilots after a specified number of hours in the air, plus years of service and proven command ability. It is in oxidized silver and is identical to the Senior Pilot Badge, except that the star atop the shield is completely encircled by a wreath of oak leaves in silver.

27. Combat (Aircraft) Observer

This badge was authorized on November 10, 1941, for aircraft observers specially trained for combat duty (which meant that the man was a qualified gunner). It is of oxidized silver and is the same as the Airplane Observer Badge approved on October 14, 1921.

28. Technical Observer Badge

This badge was authorized on November 10, 1941, for qualified personnel and trained observers, not qualified as gunners but with special training in aerial photography. It is the usual style of oxidized silver badge, with spread wings, in the center of which appears the letter "O" in front of the letter "T."

29. Balloon Pilot Badge

Authorized on November 10, 1941. This badge is identical to the Balloon Observer Badge and the Military Aeronaut Badge; only the title was changed. The badge is oxidized silver, regulation size.

30. Senior Balloon Pilot Badge

Authorized on November 10, 1941, for balloon pilots with a specified number of hours in the air plus years of service. It is identical to the Balloon Pilot Badge, with the addition of a five-pointed silver star, one point up, centered atop the balloon.

31. Balloon Observer Badge

Authorized on November 10, 1941. It is an oxidized silver badge of the usual style, exactly like the Balloon Pilot Badge in appearance, with the addition of the letter "O" in front of the balloon, also in silver.

32. Service Pilot Badge

This badge was authorized on September 4, 1942, for service pilots. It is an oxidized silver badge of the usual style with spread wings, in the center of which appears a shield, and centered on it is the letter "S."

33. Glider Pilot Badge

This badge was authorized on September 4, 1942, for trained glider pilots. This oxidized silver badge has the usual style of spread wings, in the center of which appears a shield like that of the Service Pilot Badge. In the center of the shield appears the letter "G."

34. Liaison Pilot Badge

This badge was authorized on September 4, 1942, for trained liaison pilots of the USAAF. It is oxidized silver, and identical to the Service Pilot Badge and the Glider Pilot Badge, except that in the center of the shield is the letter "L."

35. Bombardier Badge

This badge was authorized on September 4, 1942, for qualified aerial bombardiers. It is an oxidized silver badge of the usual style, with spread wings, in the center is a drop bomb, point down, superimposed on a circular target.

36. Navigator Badge

This badge was authorized on September 4, 1942, for qualified aerial navigators of the USAAF. It is an oxidized silver badge of the usual style with spread wings, in the center of which appears an armillary, or ringed sphere.

37. Air Crew Member Badge

This badge was authorized on September 4, 1942, for air crew members not covered by any of the other types of badges. It is an oxidized silver badge of the usual style with spread wings, in the center of which appears the Coat of Arms of the United States in a circular form.

38. Flight Surgeon Badge

This badge was authorized on February 11, 1943, for Medical Corps officers who were rated as flight surgeons only while they were on duty with the Air Corps. It has the usual style of spread wings, in the center of which appears the insigne of the Medical Corps, the caduceus, centered upon an oval. The wings of the caduceus extend above the wings' tops. These badges are gold-plated.

39. Aerial Gunner Badge

This badge was authorized on April 29, 1943, for qualified

29

30

31

32

33

34

35

36

37

38

aerial gunners and aerial armament technicians. It is in oxidized silver, with the usual style of spread wings, in the center of which appears a winged bullet, point down.

40. **Flight Nurse Badge**

Authorized on December 15, 1943. This badge is gold and is exactly like the Flight Surgeon Badge, except that it is smaller, only 2 inches in width, whereas all the other badges are about 3⅛ inches wide. The letter "N" is superimposed and centered on the caduceus.

Flight Surgeon and **Flight Nurse Badges** (**Second Style**)

Authorized on September 12, 1944. Both these badges were changed from gold to silver to conform to the standards of the other badges. The designs and sizes of both badges remained the same.

Combat Flight Duty Patch

This badge was authorized on February 20, 1943, for wear under aviation badges to indicate a current assignment to combat flight duty in a combat area. When the individual left the combat area, the patch was removed. It is a patch of dark blue cloth, 1¼ inches by 3¼ inches. (Not shown.)

In 1947, when the United States Air Force was created, apart from the Army, to become a separate branch of service, the United States Army anticipated that certain flying assignments would still have to be handled by it. These assignments included the use of light planes for artillery spotting, and, of course, the use of what was then a rather new weapon, the helicopter. The Korean War and the Cold War certainly proved the expectation to be correct.

Because the Air Force retained most of the badges it had used while it was part of the Army, the Army decided to adopt new aviation badges.

41. **Army Aviator Badge**

This badge was authorized for qualified military pilots of the United States Army. It is 2¾ inches wide, and comprises two well-designed upswept wings with a shield like the

39

40

41

42

43

44

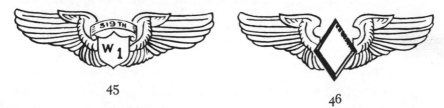

45

46

Presidential Seal at the center of the wings. The whole badge is carried out in silver.

42. Senior Army Aviator

This is identical to the Army Aviator Badge, but with the addition of a silver five-pointed star, with one point up, centered directly over the shield. It was authorized for qualified army aviators with a specified number of hours in the air and years of service.

43. Master Army Aviator

This is identical to the Senior Army Aviator Badge but with the addition of a wreath of laurel which completely encircles the star atop the shield. The badge is silver. It was authorized for qualified senior Army aviators who attained a specified number of hours in the air, plus a specified number of years of service and proven command ability.

44. Army Aviation Medical Officer

This badge, in silver, is shaped like the Army Aviator Badge, except for the shield in the center. Though the shape is retained, it bears the symbol of medicine, the staff of Aesculapius. This badge is authorized for medical officers of the Army attached to and serving with flying groups.

The next two badges are those of the Women's Air Force service pilots and the women ferry pilots who served so well during World War II flying in noncombat jobs for the Army Air Force.

45. Women's Air Force Service Pilots

These silver wings were regulation size. The twin wings have a small shield at the center and a scroll above. In the illustration, "319" stands for the 319th Training Detachment, and the "W 1" indicates the first class to graduate under the Women's Flying Training Program.

46. Women's Army Service Pilot

This badge was the one usually worn by the women pilots. It is all silver and regulation size with spread wings, in the center of which appears a diamond shape also in silver. It was authorized for the women service pilots of the United

States Army who had passed a qualifying test and were actually flying noncombat missions for the Army during World War II.

In 1947, the United States Army Air Force (USAAF), which had grown to such great proportions during World War II, was made a separate service, the United States Air Force. The Air Force continued to use the badges which were authorized under USAAF regulations, but it also created some new badges.

AIR FORCE BADGES

47. Pilot Badge
This is identical to the pilot badge of the USAAF. It comprises two spread wings, bearing an American shield in the center, and is of oxidized silver. It is authorized for qualified pilots of the Air Force.

48. Senior Pilot Badge
This is identical to the Senior Pilot Badge of the USAAF. The badge, in oxidized silver, is the same as the Pilot Badge with the addition of a five-pointed silver star with one point up centered above the shield. It is authorized for pilots with a specified number of hours in the air and a specified number of years of service.

49. Command Pilot Badge
This is identical to the Command Pilot Badge of the USAAF. The badge, in oxidized silver, is the same as the Senior Pilot Badge, with the exception that the star atop the shield is completely encircled by a wreath of oak leaves, in silver. It is authorized for senior pilots with a specified number of hours in the air, a specified number of years of service, and proven command ability.

50. Pilot Astronaut
The badge, in oxidized silver, is identical to the Pilot's Badge, with the exception that a symbol of a star is shown passing through an oval representing an earth-orbit circle.

47

48

49

50

51

52

53

54

55

This symbol is superimposed upon the shield in the center of the spread wings. The badge is authorized for pilots who are qualified to pilot powered vehicles capable of flights more than fifty miles from the earth's surface and who have made at least one such flight.

51. **Senior Pilot Astronaut**

    The badge, in oxidized silver, is identical to the Pilot Astronaut Badge, with the addition of a five-pointed star, one point up, centered above the shield. The badge is authorized for senior pilots who meet the same conditions needed to qualify as a pilot astronaut. If the astronaut was a senior pilot prior to his fifty-mile-high flight, his new rating would be that of a senior pilot astronaut.

52. **Command Pilot Astronaut**

    The badge, in oxidized silver, is identical to the Senior Pilot Astronaut Badge, with the exception that the star atop the shield is completely encircled by a wreath of oak leaves in silver. The badge is authorized for command pilots who qualify as astronauts by meeting the conditions necessary to qualify as a pilot astronaut. If the astronaut was a command pilot prior to his fifty-mile-high flight, his new rating would be that of command pilot astronaut.

53. **Navigator** and **Aircraft Observer**

    This badge, in silver, consists of the usual type of spread wings in the center of which appears the metal shield of the Air Force Seal and the Seal itself. The badge is the regulation 3 inches wide. The badge is authorized for qualified navigators and aircraft observers.

54. **Senior Navigator** and **Senior Aircraft Observer**

    The silver badge is identical to the Navigator or Aircraft Observer Badge, but with the addition of a five-pointed star, one point up, centered directly above the shield. It is authorized for qualified navigators or aircraft observers with a specified number of hours in the air and a specified number of years' service.

55. **Master Navigator** and **Master Aircraft Observer**

    The badge, in silver, is identical to that of the senior navi-

56

57

58

59

60

61

62

gator or senior aircraft observer, but with the addition of a wreath of oak leaves that completely encircle the star atop the shield. It is authorized for senior navigators or senior aircraft observers with a specified number of hours in the air and a specified number of years' service.

56. Air Crew Member

This is identical to the Air Crew Member Badge of the USAAF. The badge, in silver, has the usual style of spread wings, at the center of which appears the Coat of Arms of the United States in a circular form. It is authorized for airmen who form part of flying crews and for ground repair personnel.

57. Senior Air Crew Member

This is identical to the Air Crew Member Badge, but with the addition of a five-pointed silver star, one point up, centered directly above the circular Coat of Arms of the United States, which appears in the center. It is authorized for air crew members with a specified number of years of service.

58. Chief Air Crew Member

This is identical to the Senior Air Crew Member Badge, but with the addition of the star atop the coat of arms, which is completely encircled by a wreath of laurel leaves. It is authorized for a senior air crew member with a specified number of hours in the air, a number of years' service, and a number of qualifying tests.

59. Flight Surgeon Badge

This badge, in silver, consists of the usual spread wings, in the center of which is an outline shield from the Air Force Seal. In the center of the shield appears the symbol of medicine, the staff of Aesculapius. This badge is authorized for all medical doctors in the Air Force, regardless of flight time. Many of the flight surgeons in the Air Force are involved in important research work.

60. Senior Flight Surgeon

This badge is identical to the Flight Surgeon Badge, but with the addition of a five-pointed star, one point up, centered directly above the shield at the center of the wings.

It is authorized for flight surgeons who have completed a specified number of years of service.

61. **Chief Flight Surgeon**

This badge, in silver, is identical to the Senior Flight Surgeon Badge, but with the exception that a scroll pattern in silver appears at the top of the shield and in back of the star. This badge is authorized for senior flight surgeons who have completed a specified number of years of service.

62. **Flight Nurse Badge**

This is identical to the Flight Surgeon Badge, except that the symbol of medicine, the staff of Aesculapius, is superimposed over a burning Florence Nightingale lamp to indicate that the badge is for nurses. This is the only Air Force aviation badge which is not the regulation 3 inches long; it is 2 inches long.

NAVY, MARINE CORPS, AND COAST GUARD AVIATION BADGES

63. **Naval Aviator, Marine Corps Pilot,** and
Coast Guard Pilot Badge

This badge, the same for all three services, is gold-colored. The badge is about 2¾ inches long. It comprises two rather well-designed wings bearing, at the center, an American shield, which is in turn superimposed upon a fouled anchor. These "wings" have been in use since the very beginning of naval aviation and have never been changed in design or color. The original wings were 14-carat gold.

64. **Naval Aviation Observer**

This badge, which is authorized for the Navy and Marine Corps only, is the same size as the Naval Aviator Badge. The badge has two spread wings in gold, in the center of which appears a circle in silver, in which appears an anchor in silver. Behind this is an area filled in with gold. The anchor is unusual because it is open, rather than fouled or with a cable. The badge is authorized for qualified aviation observers.

63

64

65

66

67

68

69

70

65. Balloon Pilot

This badge is authorized for the Navy and the Marine Corps only for qualified balloon pilots and pilots of the Naval Lighter-than-Air Service. The badge is gold and is identical to the Naval Aviator badges, except that the wing to the wearer's right is removed, creating a half wing.

66. Naval Flight Surgeon (Obsolete)

This badge is authorized for the Navy and the Coast Guard only. It is rather large and has two modern-style spread wings, in the center of which is an oval. In the oval is a large oak leaf with an acorn in the center, the naval symbol for the Medical Corps. The whole badge is carried out in gold, except for the acorn, which is in silver. This badge is authorized for all flight surgeons. It is not authorized for the Marine Corps because as part of the Navy, the Corps has no doctors and relies upon the naval medical staff.

67. Air Crew Member

This badge is authorized for the Navy, Marine Corps, and Coast Guard. It is smaller than most, only 1¾ inches wide. It has two sharply upswept silver wings. In the center of the wings is a gold-colored circular badge with a fouled anchor therein. Below the circular area is a scroll bearing the words "Air Crew" in silver, and above the circular center is a scroll in silver in which are placed stars in gold. Three stars is the maximum number worn. One star each is worn to indicate that the air crewman engaged enemy aircraft; engaged enemy combatant vessels; and bombed enemy fortified positions. The author has always seen these badges with all three stars in place, so it could be that the original meaning of the stars was lost and they became a symbolic part of the design.

68. Air Crew Member (Second Style)

This badge, in gold, is authorized for the Navy and the Marine Corps. It is the regulation size, 2¾ inches wide, and was designed to bring the Air Crew Member Badge into a more uniform style than the previous badge (67). It is rather like the Naval Aviation Observer Badge, with two spread wings. In the center of these is a circle. Within the circle is a plain straight anchor; to the left of the anchor is the letter "A," and to the right is the letter "C," for Air Crew.

69. **Naval Astronaut Pilot's Badge**

This badge is identical to the Naval Aviator's Badge (63) with the addition of a symbol of a star shown passing through an oval representing an earth-orbit circle. This symbol is superimposed upon the shield in the center of the spread wings, the whole of which is superimposed upon a fouled anchor. The badge is completely gold-colored. These wings are authorized for pilots who are qualified to pilot powered vehicles capable of flights more than fifty miles above the earth's surface, and who have made at least one such flight. These wings were earned by Colonel John Glenn of the Marine Corps in addition to the following badge.

70. **Marine Corps Astronaut Insigne**

This badge might be considered a special presentation insigne. It was presented to Lieutenant Colonel John H. Glenn, Jr., America's first orbital astronaut, on March 9, 1962. The badge shows a missile in platinum, with the word "Astronaut," in gold, running the length of the missile. At the top of the missile is a replica of a space capsule, with swept-back wings added to the badge for design balance. Behind the missile is a replica of the earth, with the globe and wings also in gold. Photos of Glenn wearing this badge show him wearing it on his right breast instead of the left, as is customary.

71. **Navy** and **Marine Corps Parachutist Badge**

This badge, in silver, is authorized for qualified personnel who have passed certain requirements to become qualified parachutists. It is 1½ inches long. At the center is an open parachute flanked on either side by sculptured wings curving up and inward so as to join the tips thereof to the edge of the parachute canopy. This badge is identical in design to the Army badge, and personnel who have earned the Army badge may wear this badge if they enlist in the Navy or Marine Corps.

Navy and **Marine Corps Basic Parachutist Badge**
This badge is identical to the aforementioned badge (71).
Only the title was changed with the adoption of the "new"
parachutist badge.

72. Navy and **Marine Corps Parachutist Badge** (**New**)
This badge is awarded to personnel previously qualified for
the basic Parachutist Badge, after they have completed
certain additional required parachute jumps and/or time in
grade. This badge is gold, and is 2¾ inches wide. It has the
same type of spread wings as used on the Naval Aviator
Badge, except that a gold-colored open parachute is centered on the wings instead of the shield and fouled anchor.

OTHERS

73. **Submarine Officer's Badge**
This badge is authorized for officers of the "silent service,"
the submarine branch of the United States Navy. It is a gold
badge worn above the left breast pocket. In the center is a
bow view of a submarine proceeding on the surface, with
bow rudders rigged for diving, flanked by decorative dolphins in horizontal position, with their heads resting on the
upper edges of the rudders. This is one of the most beautiful
and highly prized badges of the naval service.

74. **Submarine Combat Badge**
This badge is awarded to officers and men of the submarine
service who complete one or more patrols during which the
submarine to which they were attached sinks an enemy
vessel or accomplishes a combat mission of equal impor-
tance. The design shows a submarine on the surface, plowing
through the water. It has decorative wave patterns at the
bottom, and centered there is a scroll. The whole badge is in
silver. Miniature gold stars may be mounted on the scroll
to indicate further awards. Three gold stars would indicate
four patrols (the badge itself would indicate the first pa-

71
72

73

74

75

76

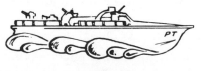

77

trol). This badge is worn on the left breast, below the line of ribbon bars for officers, and above the ribbon bars for enlisted men.

75. **Submarine Medical Officer**

This badge is authorized for medical officers and surgeons who have qualified for specialized duty aboard submarines. It is rather like the Submarine Badge, except that instead of being a submarine the center device is an oval bearing an oak leaf and acorn, the symbol of the Medical Corps. At either side of this device are facing decorative dolphins. The whole badge is gold except for the acorn, which is silver.

76. **Submarine Engineering Officer**

This badge is authorized for engineering officers of the submarine service. It is identical to the Submarine Officer's Badge, except that in the center, instead of the submarine, there is a circle in silver, in which appears a three-bladed propeller, the symbol of the engineering or machinist branch of the naval service. This also is in silver, with the background in gold. The rest of the badge is gold, and at either side of the circle are the decorative dolphins symbolic of the submarine service.

77. **Motor Torpedo Boat Badge**

This badge, though never official, was worn during World War II by personnel of the patrol torpedo (PT) boats. It shows a PT boat driving through the water, with decorative waves at the bottom. The whole badge is in silver. It was worn in the same manner as the approved Submarine Officer's Badge (73).

78. **Expert Infantryman Badge**

This badge is authorized for the Army only. The badge is awarded to officers and enlisted men "who attain established standards or whose action in combat is rated satisfactory." It was approved on November 11, 1943. The badge is worn on the left breast above the ribbon bars. It is 3 inches wide and consists of a blue enamel oblong edged in silver. Within this is an old-style infantry musket, as used on the infantry insigne.

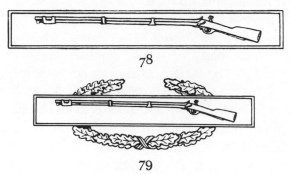

78

79

80

81

82

83

84

79. **Combat Infantryman Badge**

This badge was authorized on November 15, 1943, for officers and men of the United States Army "whose conduct in combat is exemplary or whose combat action occurs in a major action." The "CIB," as this badge is called, is highly prized in the Army, and rightfully so. It is identical to the Expert Infantryman Badge, a blue enamel oblong edged in silver, in which appears an early-style infantry musket, but with the addition of a silver wreath of oak leaves, on which the oblong is placed. The wreath is open at the top.

80. **Combat Infantryman Badge, Second Award**

This is identical to the Combat Infantryman Badge, with addition of a five-pointed silver star, with one point up, centered above the oblong and between the wreath.

81. **Combat Infantryman Badge, Third Award**

This is identical to the Combat Infantryman Badge, with the addition of two five-pointed stars, one point up. They are side by side and centered above the blue enamel oblong, with the outer points of the stars joining the wreath.

82. **Combat Infantryman Badge, Fourth Award**

This is identical to the Combat Infantryman Badge, with the addition of three five-pointed stars, one point up. The center star is slightly higher than the ones at either side, and the whole pattern is centered above the enameled oblong. The stars join with the wreath at their points.

83. **Explosive Ordnance Disposal Badge**

This badge is authorized for Army personnel qualified as ordnance or explosive disposal specialists; it is also known as the Bomb Specialist Badge. In the center is a drop shape, in which appear four bolts of lightning. An airplane bomb with point down and fins up is superimposed upon this design. The whole design is in turn placed upon a wreath of laurel leaves, which is open at the top. The complete badge is carried out in oxidized silver. It is worn on the left breast.

84. **Explosive Ordnance Disposal Supervisor Badge**

This badge is authorized for qualified explosive ordnance disposal specialists with a specified period in grade or years of service. It is identical to the Specialist Badge, with the addition of a five-pointed silver star, one point up, which appears centered upon the body of the bomb.

85. **Army Parachutist Badge**

This badge, in silver, is authorized for personnel who have passed certain tests and met educational standards for qualified parachutists. It is 1½ inches long. In the center is an open parachute flanked on either side by beautifully sculptured wings curving up and inward, and joining their tips to the edge of the parachute canopy.

86. **Senior Parachutist Badge**

This badge is authorized for qualified parachutists with a specified number of jumps and years of service. It is in silver and is identical to the Parachutist Badge, with the addition of a silver five-pointed star centered directly atop the parachute canopy.

87. **Master Parachutist Badge**

This badge is authorized for wear by senior parachutists who have attained a certain number of jumps, years of service, plus proven command ability. It is in silver and identical to the Senior Parachutist Badge, with the addition of a wreath of laurel leaves which completely encircles the star atop the parachute canopy.

88. **Army Glider Badge**

This badge, in silver, was authorized March 14, 1944, for personnel specially trained in gliders, the glider troops, and supporting units. It was authorized for wear by any person who had made at least one combat drop with a glider-borne unit. The wing is the central design and the tips sweep up and inward. Resting upon the wings in the center is a glider. The similarity between this badge and the Parachutist Badge has a special meaning, for the glider-borne troops and paratroops operated under the same command during World War II.

89. **Salvage Diver Badge**

This badge was authorized on February 15, 1944, for personnel of the Army who have qualified as deep-sea salvage divers. In silver, it shows a replica of a diver's helmet (hard hat) as used in deep-sea diving. Centered on the neck piece of the helmet is the letter "S." The badge is worn on the left breast of the uniform, below the ribbon bars.

90. **Second-Class Diver Badge**

This badge was authorized for the Army on February 15, 1944, for those who have passed a certain series of requirements or attended a specialized school for divers. It is identical to the Salvage Diver Badge, except that no letter "S" appears on the neck piece. It is in silver and shows a diver's helmet as used for deep-sea diving. It is 1 inch deep and worn on the left breast of the uniform pocket below the ribbon bars.

91. **First-Class Diver Badge**

This badge was authorized on February 15, 1944, for qualified second-class divers with a specified number of dives, qualifying tests, and years of service. It is identical to the Second-Class Diver Badge, a deep-sea diving helmet, except that the helmet is flanked on either side by decorative dolphins. Their faces join at the bottom of the neck piece of the helmet, and their fins extend above the helmet's crown.

92. **Master Diver Badge**

This badge was authorized on February 15, 1944, for first-class divers with a certain number of dives, plus years of service and proven command ability. It is identical to the First-Class Diver Badge, a silver diver's helmet flanked on either side by dolphins, except that the helmet is resting upon a trident. The whole badge is 1¼ inches high, and it is worn on the left breast of the uniform, below the ribbon bars.

93. **Combat Medical Badge**

This badge, in silver, is authorized for medical personnel "who attain established standards or whose action in combat is exemplary or occurs in a major action." It has the insigne of the Medical Corps, the staff or caduceus, at the top of which appears a cross, as used on the arm band of the Medical Corps. This in turn is centered upon a stretcher.

85

86

87

88

89

90

91

92

93

94

95

96

97

98

The whole is enclosed by a wreath of oak leaves, open at the top. The badge is worn upon the left breast of the uniform, above the ribbon bars.

Medical Badge

This badge, the same as the Combat Medical Badge (93) but without the wreath, is awarded to qualified medical personnel who have not served in combat.

94. **Army Medical Badge, Second Award**

This is identical to the Combat Medical Badge, with the addition of a five-pointed silver star centered above the cross, between the wings of the caduceus.

95. **Combat Medical Badge, Third Award**

This is identical to the Combat Medical Badge, with the addition of two five-pointed stars, one point up, at the top of the cross and at the bottom of the caduceus. Both are centered, and the whole badge is in silver.

96. **Combat Medical Badge, Fourth Award**

This is identical to the Combat Medical Badge, with the addition of three five-pointed silver stars, which appear with one point up. One appears at either end of the stretcher, centered between the handles and upon the wreath; the third star appears centered above the cross, between the wings of the caduceus. The whole badge is in silver.

97. **Combat Field Artillery Badge**

This badge, though unofficial, has been worn on Army uniforms. It is similar to the Combat Infantryman's Badge. It is an oblong, enameled red, and edged in silver, at the center of which appear crossed cannon, the insigne of the artillery. The red in the enamel is the color of the artillery. The whole badge rests upon a wreath of oak leaves, open at the top and centered in back of the oblong. It is believed that the same requirements of the Combat Infantryman Badge must have been met in the artillery to merit this badge.

98. **Combat Armored Cavalry Badge**

This badge, also unofficial, has been worn on the uniform. It is also similar to the Combat Infantryman Badge, and it is believed to have been awarded for the same type of action but in the armored cavalry. The badge consists of an oblong in yellow enamel, edged in silver, in the center of which appear crossed cavalry sabers. In the center of this is a tank, front view. This is the insigne of the armored cavalry and yellow is the color of the cavalry. The whole rests upon a wreath of oak leaves, open at the top and centered behind the oblong.

99. USAF Parachutist Badge

This badge is authorized for qualified parachutists of the Air Force. It is rather small, about an inch in depth. The badge is worn on the left breast above the ribbon bars. The badge is in the shape of a shield taken from the Air Force Seal. The badge is silver-colored at the bottom, and where the cloud line begins, it becomes light blue enamel, as in the Air Force colors. Centered upon the shield is an open parachute in white enamel.

100. USAF Senior Parachutist Badge

This is identical to the Parachutist Badge, with the addition of a five-pointed silver star that appears centered atop the shield. This badge is awarded to qualified parachutists with a specified number of jumps, tests, and years of service.

101. USAF Master Parachutist Badge

This is identical to the Senior Parachutist Badge, with the addition of a white enameled scroll pattern that appears atop the shield and in back of the silver star. It is awarded to senior parachutists with a specified number of jumps, years of service, and proven command ability in this particular specialty.

102. USAF Nurses' Badge

This badge is authorized for nurses of the Air Force and is worn above the row of ribbon bars on all uniforms except the dress uniform. It is a shield taken from the coat of arms of the USAF. The shield is in light blue enamel, edged in silver, and has a caduceus at the center. Behind this is the lamp of Florence Nightingale.

99

100

101

102

103

104

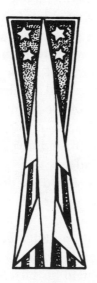

105

106

103. **USAF Dentists' Badge**
This badge is identical to the nurses' badge, but without the lamp of Florence Nightingale. Instead the letter "D" appears in front of the staff. It is worn in the same manner as the nurses' badge by qualified dentists of the Air Force.

104. **USAF Physicians' Badge**
This badge, which is identical to the Dentists' Badge, but without the "D," is worn in the same manner by qualified physicians serving with the Air Force. It is worn above the ribbon bars on all uniforms except the dress uniform.

105. **USAF Guided Missile Badge**
This badge is authorized for trained and qualified personnel of the Air Force who serve in the guided missile arm, and to anyone guarding or assisting this job. Worn on the left breast below the pocket, it consists of a silver missile in flight, nose up. It is set upon an oxidized silver background, with two stars displayed on either side of the upper part of the missile. The lower part of the badge is separated into sections to indicate vapor trails.

106. **Identification, Guard, Tomb of the Unknown Soldier**
This well-designed badge, authorized for members of the Honor Guard at the Tomb of the Unknown Soldier in Washington, D.C., is worn on the right breast pocket of the uniform. It is made of frosted and cut silver with the highlights chased to a high brilliance and is composed of an inverted wreath of laurel and olive leaves intertwined at the top. Upon the wreath is a replica of the side of the Tomb itself on a raised platform. On the platform appear the words "Honor Guard" in two lines. The badge is frosted silver.

107. **Department of Defense Identification Badge**
This badge, authorized for personnel assigned to duty in the Defense Department, is worn on the upper left pocket, below the ribbon bars. It is not worn after an individual is detached from such duty. This identification badge consists of a gold spread eagle, grasping three gold, crossed arrows. Below, centered upon the eagle, are a shield of thirteen red and white stripes and a blue chief, all in enamel. Passing

behind the wing tips are a gold amulet bearing thirteen gold stars above the eagle and a wreath of laurel and olive in green enamel below the eagle. The whole design is superimposed on a circular, cut-silver sunburst of thirty-three rays. The badge is 2 inches wide.

108. **White House Service Badge**

This badge is authorized for personnel assigned to duty at the White House. It is worn on the upper right pocket of the uniform, but may not be worn after the individual is detached from such duty. The badge is a 2-inch white enamel disk, in the center of which appears the center device of the Presidential Seal without its surrounding stars, in silver. The whole design is surrounded by twenty-seven gold rays from the center and a circular band in gold. The badge is 2¼ inches in diameter.

109. **Joint Chiefs of Staff Identification Badge**

This badge is authorized for any member of the Armed Forces who has been assigned to the Organization of the Joint Chiefs of Staff and served not less than one year. It may not be worn after the individual is detached from such service. The badge is worn on the left pocket of the uniform, below the ribbon bars. The badge has a shield of the United States, with the chief in blue enamel and the thirteen alternating stripes of white and red enamel, superimposed on four gold-colored unsheathed swords, two in pale and two in saltier with points to the chief. The blades and grips of the swords are entwined with a gold-metal continuous scroll surrounding the shield with the word "Joint" at the top and the words "Chiefs of Staff" at the bottom. This is all in blue enamel, and the whole design is within an oval silver metal wreath of laurel leaves. The badge is 2¼ inches in overall width.

110. **Department of the Army General Staff Identification Badge**

This badge was created under personal direction of General Douglas MacArthur, then Chief of Staff, and was authorized on August 23, 1933. It is awarded to officers of the Army who, since June 1920, have served not less than one year on

107

108

109

110

the General Staff or have received a certificate of eligibility from the War Department. It was originally called the War Department General Staff Badge. The badge is worn centered on the upper right breast pocket of the uniform coat. It has the Coat of Arms of the United States in gold in the center. The centered shield consists of the chief, in blue enamel, and the thirteen alternating stripes of white and red enamel. The cloud above is in blue enamel, and the thirteen stars are in white enamel. The Coat of Arms is centered upon a five-pointed star, one point up, in black enamel edged in gold. Between the arms of the star appear olive and laurel leaves in light green enamel, with gold balls separating the leaves. The badge of the Chief of Staff and former chiefs of staff is 3 inches in diameter; for others, the badge is 2 inches.

The following five badges are of recent issue.

111. Flight Surgeon Insigne, Navy (New)
This badge, which replaced the badge previously mentioned, is of the usual size in gold-colored metal or gold-embroidered. The badge has two spread wings with an oval center design, upon which appears the Medical Corps device, a gold oak leaf with a silver acorn in its center. The badge measures 2¾ inches from wing tip to wing tip.

112. Flight Nurse Insigne, Navy
This badge is the same design as that prescribed for flight surgeon, except that there is no silver acorn in the center and it is slightly smaller, only 2 inches from wing tip to wing tip. The oak leaf without the acorn is the emblem of the Navy Medical Service Corps.

113. Command at Sea Insigne
A gold-colored metal pin consisting of a five-pointed pyramid-shaped star superimposed on anchor flukes and a partially unfurled commission pennant showing six stars, each with one ray pointing up. The insigne is 1½ inches in diameter.

111

112

113

114

115

116

117

118

119

The Command at Sea Insigne is worn as follows: Officers currently in command at sea wear the insigne on the right breast centered immediately above the pocket, except on mess jackets and evening dress blue coat, when it is worn centered on the lapel. When a unit commendation ribbon is worn on the right breast, the insigne is centered below the ribbon. Officers having previously held commands at sea (but not currently in command), wear the insignia on the left breast, centered below ribbons, medals, and other insignia. When the insignia is worn alone, it shall be worn centered above the pocket. If the Department of Defense Badge is worn, the Command at Sea badge shall be worn uppermost.

114. Submarine Supply Corps Insigne

This insigne is the same size as the Submarine Officer's Badge, in gold-colored metal. It is authorized for qualified officers of the supply corps serving in the submarine service. The badge has two dolphins facing a center design of the supply corps, an oak leaf, which is the same as the collar device of this corps.

115. Air Force Combat Crew Badge

This badge, in silver, is authorized for Air Force personnel who have served or are serving as crewmen in a combat zone. The badge is a rectangular frame, 2¾ inches wide by ½ inch high. At the left is the emblem of the Air Force, and at the right, the words "Combat Crew" in a block form. The letters, emblem, and frame are in polished silver and the background in pebbled frosted silver. It is worn in the same manner as the pilots' badges of the Air Force.

There is no official reference to the following four badges, but they might very well have been in use for a short period of time.

116. Navy Navigator Badge

This badge consists of two rather well-designed half wings in gold, bearing in the center a trophy consisting of two crossed fouled anchors in gold. Centered upon the anchors is a silver circle, which usually looks black, and centered in the circle is a compass rose, in gold. The badge is 2¾ inches from wing tip to wing tip. It was probably authorized for qualified naval navigators just prior to World War II.

117. Air Rescue Personnel Badge

This badge, in silver, is similar to the qualification badges of the Air Force. It consists of the usual spread wings, in the center of which is an outline of a shield from the Air Force Seal. In the center of the shield appears an upright ladder, and centered upon the ladder, two crossed fireman's axes, as used in rescue work. The center design seems to be symbolic of rescue work.

118. Flight Engineer Badge

This badge, in silver, is identical to the World War II–style pilots' wings, with the exception that the center shield is replaced by an old-style airplane engine with a four-bladed propeller centered upon the engine. This badge was probably authorized for qualified flight engineers of the United States Army Air Corps during World War II.

119. Glider Troop Badge

This badge, in silver, was probably the original badge used for glider-trained personnel early in World War II. It is 1½ inches long and is very like the Army Parachutist Badge, an open parachute flanked by upswept curved wings, the tips joining at the top of the parachute canopy. Centered upon these wings is an Army-type glider, front view. This badge was discontinued with the adoption of the present Army Glider Badge, which was authorized on March 14, 1944.

PART III

Shooting and Marksmanship Badges

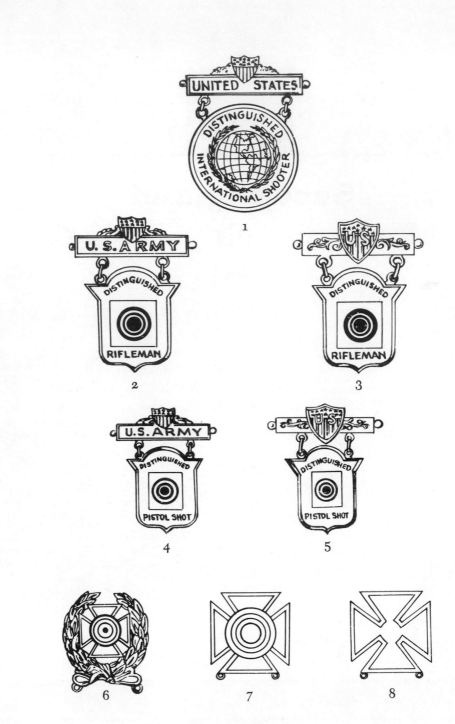

1

2

3

4

5

6

7

8

THIS SECTION DEALS with the qualification and award badges given specifically for marksmanship and gunnery. These are commonly called "shooting medals," as the majority of them are awarded for just that — shooting. They are awarded to members of the military service for some special proficiency or skill. They consist of a medallion hung from a bar or bars, and are awarded in gold, silver, and bronze for different grades of proficiency. They are worn on the military uniform, directly below all ribbon bars on the left breast. If worn alone, they are to be worn with the top or suspension bar directly above the top of the pocket flap. There are, however, certain exceptions, such as the Navy's Expert Rifleman and Expert Pistol Shot medals, and the Coast Guard's Expert Rifleman and Expert Pistol Shot badges. Though indeed they are badges, their specifications make them medals, because the medal pendant hangs from a regulation-size ribbon. They are awarded with separate ribbon bar attachments, which are worn as ribbon bars alone on most uniforms. The medals themselves are worn along with all regulation-size medals on special occasions, when all regulation-size medals and decorations are worn.

This section deals only with the "official" shooting and qualification badges. There are a great number of shooting awards made to military personnel by various organizations, but they are not authorized for wear on the military uniform. There are, in fact, enough of this type of award to justify a book on that subject alone.

The Distinguished International Shooter Badge is authorized for all branches of the military, and it is the same badge for all services. This is the highest badge of distinction that can be awarded to a member of the military, and it takes precedence over all badges awarded for shooting by members of the military services.

The highest badges awarded by each of the military services are the Distinguished Marksman or Rifleman badges and the Distinguished Pistol Shot Badge. These are the same for all the branches, and the only difference is the top suspension bar, which has the name of the service of which the individual is a member when the badge is awarded. The bars read either "U.S. Army," "U.S. Navy," "U.S. Marine Corps," "U.S. Coast Guard," or "U.S. Air Force." If a member of the Marine Corps, for example, had been awarded a Distinguished Marksman Badge and then left this branch to join another, say the Army, he would wear the Distinguished Marksman Badge of the Marine Corps on the Army uniform, and would not automatically be awarded the badge of the Army. If, however, he were to continue to fire on Army teams and achieved this status with the Army, he would be entitled to an Army Distinguished Marksman Badge, but he would wear only one shooting badge on the uniform. The only exception is that both the Distinguished Marksman Badge and the Distinguished Pistol Shot Badge may be worn on the uniform simultaneously, and any such change of service might very well result in a distinguished shooter's wearing one of each badge from different branches of the military on his uniform.

The Distinguished Marksman badges are awarded to personnel who, as shooting members of a winning team, have won any three badges in any of the following events: divisional rifle or pistol matches, all-service rifle or pistol matches, national trophy individual matches, and/or national trophy team matches.

The Marine Corps awards the largest number of badges of any one service. This is because the Marine Corps puts much more emphasis upon shooting than do any of the other branches of the military. Then too, it awards badges to correspond with each of the individual or team trophies and authorizes them for wear on the uniform. In other words, each man who wins a major shooting trophy or who is a member of the winning team in a team trophy match is awarded a shooting badge. The only exception is the General Shepherd Trophy.

All the other services have certain shooting trophies, but they do not have authorized badges to signify that a shooter has won or has been a member of the winning team for such a trophy.

This section does not deal with trophies, but it pictures and describes each shooting badge.

ARMY MARKSMANSHIP AND QUALIFICATION BADGES

1. **Distinguished International Shooter**

   This badge, in gold, is awarded to distinguished marksmen of the military who have fired in international matches such as the Olympics and who have qualified as distinguished shooters. The badge consists of a bar and a circular pendant. The suspension bar has the words "United States" on it. It is rectangular in shape, and has balls at the ends. Centered at the top of the bar is a shield of the United States with a floral pattern at either edge. Suspended below this by rings is a circular plaque, and centered in this is a projection map, showing the Western Hemisphere. The whole is encircled by a wreath of olive leaves. Above this is the word "Distinguished" and below it, completing the circular pattern, are the words "International Shooter." The reverse is blank for the engraving of the recipient's name and the date of the award. The award is the same for all services.

2. **Army Distinguished Rifleman**

   This badge, in gold, is awarded to all Army personnel and personnel of the Army Reserve who have attained the status of Distinguished Marksman with the rifle in competitive matches. The badge is a shield-shaped plaque in gold, in the center of which appears an enameled target in black and white. Above this the word "Distinguished" appears, and below the plaque, the word "Rifleman." This is suspended from a bar, which has centered at the top a U.S. shield with a floral design at either side. On the bar appears "U.S. Army." The reverse is plain, and the name, rank, and date of the award are engraved thereon.

3. **Army Distinguished Rifleman, for Civilian Awardees**

This badge is awarded to civilians who have attained distinguished rifleman status firing in United States Army competitive matches. The badge is identical to the Army Distinguished Rifleman Badge, with the only difference being the bar suspension. The bar has a rather large United States Shield centered upon it, and in the shield the letters U.S. On either side of the shield is a decorative scroll pattern within the bar. This badge was the original Army Distinguished Rifleman Badge.

4. **Army Distinguished Pistol Shot**

This badge, in gold, is awarded to all Army and Army Reserve personnel who have attained the status of distinguished pistol shots in competitive Army matches. It is a gold shield-shaped plaque, in the center of which appears an enameled target in black and white; above this, the word "Distinguished," appears and below it, the words "Pistol Shot." This is suspended from a bar centered at the top of which is a United States shield, with a floral design at either side. On the bar appear the words, "U.S. Army." There are gold balls at either end of the bar. The reverse is plain, and the name and rank of the recipient and date of the award are engraved thereon. This badge is about one-third smaller than the Rifleman's Badge.

5. **Army Distinguished Pistol Shot, for Civilian Awardees**

This badge is awarded to civilians who have achieved status as distinguished pistol shots while firing in competitive Army matches. It is identical to the Distinguished Pistol Shot Badge, but the suspension bar is different. The bar has a rather large United States shield centered upon it, and in the shield are the letters "U.S." At either side of the shield is a decorative scroll pattern within the bar. This was the original Army Distinguished Pistol Shot Badge.

6. Expert Qualification Badge

This badge is authorized for qualified personnel of the Army, Army Reserve, and National Guard. It is made of oxidized silver. It is a cross pattée with a target in the center. The whole is surrounded by a wreath of laurel leaves tied at the bottom with a bow knot. It has a ring at either edge, for attaching the bar naming the weapon with which the recipient qualified.

7. Sharpshooter Qualification Badge

This badge is authorized for qualified personnel of the Army, Army Reserve, and National Guard. It is made of oxidized silver. It is a cross pattée with a target in the center. The bottom arm of the cross has a ring at either edge, for attaching the bar with the name of the weapon with which the recipient qualified.

8. Marksman Qualification Badge

This badge is authorized for qualified personnel of the Army, Army Reserve, and National Guard. Made of oxidized silver, it is a cross pattée with small curved center points. The bottom arm of the cross has a ring at either edge for attaching the bar naming the weapon with which the recipient qualified.

9. Weapon Qualification Bars

These bars are of oxidized silver with rings at the top for attaching to the badges described above, or to the last previously earned bar, and with rings at the bottom for attaching further qualification bars. They run the gamut of military weapons from the sword to the missile. The pre–World War II bars awarded were: rifle, rifle-a, rifle-b, rifle-c, pistol-d (for different courses with these weapons), automatic rifle, machine gun, infantry howitzer, coast artillery, mines, field artillery, sword, bayonet, tank weapons, c.w.s. weapons, machine rifle, aerial gunner, aerial bomber, small bore, and grenade. The bars currently in use are: rifle, pistol, antiaircraft artillery, automatic rifle, machine gun, coast artillery, submarine mines, field artillery, tank weapons, flamethrowers, submachine gun, rocket launcher, grenade, carbine, recoilless rifle, mortar, bayonet, rifle, small bore, pistol, and missile.

10. **Army Air Forces Technician Badge**

This badge, which is no longer issued, was presented to qualified personnel of the Army Air Corps during World War II. The badge is in silver. It has an airplane gear wheel surmounted by a four-bladed propeller. The whole is encircled by a wreath of laurel leaves, with a bow knot at the bottom, with rings at either end of the bow for attaching qualification bars. The bars are similar to those used on the Basic Marksmanship badges. There were twenty-four qualification bars used, ranging from Armorer through Link Trainer Instructor and Weather Forecaster.

11. **Motor Vehicle Driver and Mechanic Badge**

This badge was authorized during World War II, for qualified personnel of the Army. It is in oxidized silver and is a cross pattée with a disk wheel and tire placed in the center. At the bottom arm of the cross are two rings for attaching the bars, as on the previous badges. The bars are "Driver — W" for wheeled vehicles, "Driver — M" for Motorcycles; "Driver — T" for track or half-track vehicles; "Driver-A" for amphibian vehicles; and "Mechanic" for automotive or allied trade mechanic.

12. **Distinguished Aerial Gunner Badge (Obsolete)**

This and the following two badges were awarded to Army personnel for a period of one year, and must therefore be considered a yearly award. They are quite distinctive, and of course very rarely seen.

The badge, in gold, has a target at the bottom, in the center of which appears an aerial bullet, with wings at either side, the same as appears upon the Aerial Gunner wings. The whole is encircled by a wreath of laurel leaves and attached to the top suspension bar by a series of rings. The top bar is shaped like a cloud bank and has the word "Distinguished." The badge was awarded to the outstanding distinguished aerial gunner for one year, and then returned to Army command.

9

10

11

12

13

14

15

16

17

18

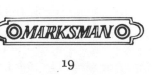

19

20

13. **Distinguished Automatic Rifleman Badge (Obsolete)**

This badge, in gold, was authorized for qualified personnel of the Army. The pendant has a target in the center, and placed horizontally in the center of the target a Browning automatic rifle. The outer edge is framed by decorative leaves that come to a point, forming a diamond shape. It has square built-up areas at either side of the target, which is attached to the suspension bar by a series of rings. The suspension bar, also in gold, has two oak leaves at either end, and centered upon the bar is the word "Distinguished." The badge was awarded to the outstanding automatic rifleman of the Army for one year, and then returned to Army command.

14. **Distinguished Aerial Bomber Badge (Obsolete)**

This badge, in gold, was authorized for qualified personnel of the Army. The pendant has a target in the center completely encircled by a wreath of laurel leaves. Superimposed upon this is an aerial bomb, point down. The fins and point of the bomb extend to the edges of the wreath. This is attached to the top suspension bar by a series of rings. The top bar is shaped like a cloud bank, with the word "Distinguished" centered upon it. The badge was awarded to the outstanding distinguished aerial bomber for one year and then returned to Army command.

15. **Corps Area Marksmanship Badge (Obsolete)**

This badge consists of three parts. It was awarded to members of a corps area marksmanship team. The pendant is in bronze, displaying in the center a crossed Indian bow and arrows within a ring bearing thirteen stars, the whole of which is surrounded by an oak wreath. There are rings at the top of the wreath for attachment of the second piece, which is known as the clasp. The clasp consists of crossed muskets for rifle teams; crossed flintlock pistols for pistol teams; or crossed Browning automatic rifles for automatic rifle teams. These clasps are in gold for first-grade shots, silver for second-grade shots, and bronze for third-grade shots. There are rings at the top of the clasps for attachment to the third piece, the suspension bar. The bar is of bronze with rounded ends, and a plain surface, with a disk in the center. In the disk appears a Roman numeral indicating the corps area, or a device indicating the department; for example, the Hawaiian Department used a dolphin, the Philippine Department, a sea lion, and the Panama Canal Department, a portcullis. The reverse of the pendant is blank, and the recipient's name, rank, and date of award were to be engraved thereon.

16. **Army Area Marksmanship Badge** (Obsolete)

This badge was awarded to members of Army marksmanship teams. It also consists of three parts. The pendant is bronze and enamel, the center displaying crossed Indian bow and arrows within a ring of enamel, bearing thirteen stars and surrounded by an oak wreath. The enameled ring is the color of the branch, blue for infantry, yellow for cavalry, red for artillery, and so on. When the branch has two colors the stars are enameled in the piping color. For the Philippine Scouts, the ring is blue and the stars are red. Clasps are the same as used on the Corps Area Marksmanship Badge. The suspension bar is in bronze with square ends and ornamented with oak leaves. The back of the pendant is blank, suitable for engraving the recipient's name and rank and the date of the award.

17. **Army Expert Rifleman Badge** (Obsolete)

This badge was awarded to Army and Army Reserve personnel who had qualified as expert in specified rifle courses. The badge, in gold-colored metal, consists of crossed rifles in front of a wreath of laurel leaves, joined at the bottom by a wreath, with the whole suspended by rings to a straight suspension bar with decorative ends. The words "Expert Rifleman" appear within the bar.

18. **Army Rifle Sharpshooter Badge** (Obsolete)

This badge was awarded to Army and Army Reserve personnel who had qualified as sharpshooter on specified rifle courses. The badge, in gold-colored metal, consists of a cross, like the cross of Malta, with the inner arms pebbled. The center of the cross is a target. This is suspended by rings from a top suspension bar with rounded ends. The word "Sharpshooter" appears within the bar.

19. **Army Rifle Marksman Badge (Obsolete)**
This badge was awarded to Army and Army Reserve personnel who had qualified as marksmen with the rifle on specified courses. The badge consists of a gold-colored framed bar with rounded ends. Within the bar appears the word "Marksman" and, at either side of this word are raised targets. The background is pebbled.

20. **Army Pistol Expert Badge (Obsolete)**
This badge was awarded to Army and Army Reserve personnel who had qualified as pistol experts. The badge, in gold-colored metal, consists of a pair of crossed "early style" service revolvers in front of a wreath of laurel leaves, which is tied at the bottom with a bow knot. This is suspended to a top bar by rings. The top bar is straight, with decorative ends, and appearing in the center are the words "Pistol Expert." A second style of this badge exists. It is the same in all respects, with the exception that the revolvers are replaced by crossed 45-caliber automatic pistols. This second style of badge is also obsolete.

NAVY MARKSMANSHIP AND QUALIFICATION BADGES

21. **Navy Distinguished Marksman Badge**
This badge, in gold, is awarded to all Navy personnel and personnel of the Naval Reserve who have attained the status of distinguished marksman with the rifle in competitive matches. It is a shield-shaped plaque in gold, in the center of which appears an enameled target in black and white. Above this is the word "Distinguished," and below it the word "Marksman." The shield is framed. This is connected to a bar by the means of rings. The suspension bar is framed, with small gold balls at either end. Within the bar appears "U.S. Navy" in raised letters. The reverse is

blank, and the name and rank of the recipient and the date of the award are engraved thereon.

22. Navy Distinguished Pistol Shot Badge

This badge, in gold, is awarded all Navy and Navy Reserve personnel who have attained the status of distinguished pistol shot in competitive matches. The badge is almost identical to the Distinguished Marksman Badge, but slightly smaller. The badge is a shield-shaped plaque in gold with a black and white enameled target in the center. Above this is the word "Distinguished," and below are the words "Pistol Shot." The plaque is framed. This is attached to a suspension bar by small rings. The bar is framed, with small gold balls at the ends, and appearing within the bar are the words "U.S. Navy." The reverse is blank and suitable for engraving.

23. Navy Expert Team Rifleman Badge (Obsolete)

This badge, in gold, was awarded to personnel of the Navy, including Marines and Naval Reserve personnel, who had qualified as expert team rifleman with the carbine or rifle, and who had fired with Naval or Marine teams in national matches. The badge shows a target in front of an anchor, with the flukes of the anchor appearing in front of the target and the top of the anchor appearing as the top of the target. This is connected to a top suspension bar by a series of rings through the eye of the anchor. The bar is straight with a rope border, which has two rope loops at the bottom. Within this bar appear the words "Expert Team Rifleman." The reverse is blank and suitable for engraving the recipient's name.

24. Navy Fleet Rifleman Badge

This badge, in gold, consists of a circular badge with an enameled target of black and white, resting on crossed rifles. At the top of the target appears the top of an anchor, and at the bottom, the feathers of an arrow. Below this appears an open wreath of laurel leaves, joined at the bottom by a bow knot. Above this are the words "Fleet Rifleman." The badge is awarded to all naval personnel who

21

22

23

24

25

26

27

28

have qualified as rifleman in a fleet match or national match. The suspension bar is the same as the Expert Team Rifleman Badge, except that the words "U.S. Navy" appear.

25. Navy Fleet Pistol Shot Badge

This badge, in gold, is awarded to naval personnel who have qualified as pistol shots in a fleet match or national match. The badge consists of a circular pendant with a black and white enameled target in the center. At the top of the target appears the top of an anchor, and below it are the feathers of an arrow. At either side of the target appear automatic pistols, all above and encircled by a wreath of laurel leaves, joined at the bottom with a bow knot. Above this appear the words "Fleet Pistol Shot." This is connected to a top suspension bar by a series of rings. The top bar has a rope border, and centered within are the words "U.S. Navy."

26. Navy Sharpshooters Medal (Obsolete)

This was the original shooting badge of the naval service. It was awarded to all personnel of the naval service who qualified as expert or sharpshooter with the pistol or rifle. The badge, of bronze, consists of a pendant disk with rope edge. In the disk is a target in front of crossed rifles; below this in a semicircle are the words "United States Navy." Overlapping the main disk is another disk containing a representation from the Navy Seal; this design shows an eagle with the United States shield on its breast, standing on an anchor. This is connected to the top suspension by a series of rings. The top bar always represents the original award. There were two different bars. One type has three ovals on a square bar, with rounded stippled ends. This is for subsequent qualifications; each such qualification is represented by a silver oval with the date upon it, which is fitted into the bronze. The second type states the reason for the award. This is similar to the top and second bars in the illustration. They are straight bars with floral patterns at the ends, and centered within these are either "Expert," "Sharpshooter," "Pistol Expert," or "Pistol Sharpshooter."

The date that the man achieved this distinction is engraved upon the bar — for instance, the illustration shows "1914." The reverses of the bars have the recipient's name, and the disk at the bottom has a blank reverse, suitable for engraving the recipient's name and the date of original award.

27. **Expert Rifleman Badge** and **Ribbon**

This award came into existence to take the place of the previous badge (26). The disk at the bottom is very similar to the previous badge. It is bronze, with a rope-border edge; overlapping this is another disk containing a representation of an eagle from the Navy Seal. The eagle has a shield on its breast, and it is perched upon an anchor. Centered on the main disk is a target, below this in a semicircle are the words "United States Navy," and above this in a straight line, are the words "Expert Rifleman." The badge is suspended by a ring to a regulation-size ribbon. The ribbon is navy blue with three very thin stripes of green. One is at the center, and the others are near either edge. The ribbon bar can be worn on the uniform in the regulation manner when medals are not worn.

28. **Expert Pistol Shot Badge** and **Ribbon**

This award was created at the same time as the previous badge, and is awarded to all personnel of the United States Navy and Naval Reserve who have qualified as expert pistol shots on specified courses. The bronze circular disk is the same as the Expert Rifleman Badge, except that the wording between the target and the overlapping disk at the top reads "Expert Pistol Shot." The badge is suspended from a regulation size ribbon by a ring at the top. The ribbon is navy blue with a very narrow stripe of light green near either edge. The ribbon bar is worn on the uniform in the prescribed manner when medals and decorations are not worn.

29. **U.S. Navy Great Guns Efficiency Medal** (**Obsolete**)

This badge, which is not official and may well have been only a pattern piece, is similar to the Expert Pistol (28) and Rifleman's (27) badge in shape. It consists of a figure-eight shape, with the top circle bearing the letter "E" surrounded by thirteen raised five-pointed stars. The bottom circular section shows a large naval warship or battleship at full steam, firing its large guns. A wake thrown up by the ship and waves are at the bottom, and along the bottom of the piece is inscribed, "United States Navy" in raised letters. The pendant is attached to a regulation-size ribbon by a ring. The ribbon is dark blue, with five narrow yellow stripes.

30. Knox Trophy Medals (**Army** and **Navy**)

These medals are presented annually by the Society of the Sons of the Revolution in Massachusetts to members of the Army and the Navy in honor of Major General Henry Knox, first Secretary of War of the United States. The obverse of the medal is same for both awards: a portrait of General Knox in Colonial uniform, facing right, with the inscription "1750–1806" and "Henry Knox" in a circular form near the edge of the medal. The reverses are as follows:

Navy Award — for Gunpointing. A figure of Columbia holding a trident and wreath, with a shield and wreath at her side, inscribed to the right, "Sons of the Revolution in Massachusetts," and in the base, "Excellence in Gunpointing." This medal is issued to the set of gunpointers of a battleship making the highest score for merit in gunnery for the preceding year.

Army Award — for Light Artillery. Crossed cannons entwined with laurel wreath on which is an eagle. Inscription at the top reads: "Society of the Sons of the Revolution in the Commonwealth of Massachusetts," and at the base of the medal "Excellence Light Artillery, U.S. Army." This medal is awarded to the sergeant of the field artillery unit attaining the highest proficiency in the preceding year.

Both medals are hung from the same ribbon, which is the regulation size, with a wide stripe of Colonial Blue in the center, flanked by wide bands of buff at the edges. This is the color of the Sons of the Revolution membership badge. At the top of the ribbon is a blank suspension bar,

29

30

31

32

33

34

35

suitable for engraving the name of the recipient, and the date of award.

The service ribbon alone may be worn upon the uniform, following all service decorations and medals in the prescribed manner.

31. Admiral Trenchard Turret-Gun-Pointer Medal

This medal is awarded annually on July 1 by the Navy League to the set of three turret pointers attaining the highest merit at short-range battle practice. The obverse, which is circular, has a set of crossed fouled anchors; centered upon this is a blue enamel medallion with a gold rope edge, within which is a vertical anchor with "U.S." in gold, and "N.L." in white. The reverse has an open wreath of laurel leaves, joined at the bottom by a bow knot; around the outer edge are the words, "Admiral Trenchard Section." At the bottom of the wreath is usually engraved the section number of the recipient. Within the wreath at the top are the words "Awarded to," and a blank space suitable for engraving the recipient's name and date of award. The medal is attached to a regulation-size ribbon by a ring; the ribbon is of blue and gold, the colors of the Navy, with a thin stripe of gold, wide band of blue, wide band of gold, and thin stripe of blue at the end. The top is in the form of a flat suspension bar, on which is engraved "Admiral Trenchard Section," with a space for engraving the recipient's section number.

COAST GUARD MARKSMANSHIP AND QUALIFICATION BADGES

32. Coast Guard Distinguished Marksman Badge

This badge is in gold and is awarded to all Coast Guard personnel who have attained the status of distinguished marksman with the rifle in competitive matches. It is a shield-shaped plaque in gold, in the center of which appears an enameled target in black and white. Above this is the word "Distinguished," and below it the word "Marksman." The shield is framed and is connected to a suspension bar by the means of rings. The suspension bar is framed, with small gold balls at either end, and within the bar appear the words, "U.S. Coast Guard" in raised letters. The reverse is blank, suitable for engraving the name and rank of the recipients and the date of award.

33. **Coast Guard Distinguished Pistol Shot Badge**

This badge, in gold, is awarded to Coast Guard personnel who have attained the status of Distinguished Pistol Shot in competitive matches. Slightly smaller than the Distinguished Marksman Badge, it is a shield-shaped plaque in gold, in the center of which appears an enameled target in black and white. Above this is the word "Distinguished," and below are the words "Pistol Shot." The shield is framed and attached to the top suspension bars by rings. The suspension bar is framed, with small gold balls at either end, and within the bar are the words "U.S. Coast Guard" in raised letters. The reverse of the badge is blank and suitable for engraving the recipient's name and rank and the date of issue of the badge.

34. **Coast Guard Expert Rifleman Badge**

This badge is, in fact, a medal, awarded to all personnel of the Coast Guard who have qualified as expert with the rifle in prescribed rifle courses. It consists of a shield-shaped pendant in bronze. The upper part has the words "U.S. Coast Guard Expert"; the lower half has crossed rifles, and below this a target. The reverse is plain, suitable for engraving the recipient's name. The badge is attached to a regulation ribbon by a ring at the top. The ribbon is navy blue with two thin white stripes in the center, and a thin white stripe near either edge. The ribbon bar can be worn alone on prescribed uniforms.

35. **Coast Guard Expert Pistol Shot Badge**

This badge, like the preceding one, is a medal. It is awarded to all personnel of the Coast Guard who have qualified as expert with the pistol on prescribed courses. The badge consists of a shield-shaped pendant in bronze. The upper part has the words "U.S. Coast Guard Expert" and in the lower half are crossed 45-caliber automatic pistols; below this is a target. The reverse is plain, suitable for engraving the recipient's name. This is attached to a regulation-size ribbon, by a ring at the top. The ribbon is navy blue, with a thin white stripe near either edge. The ribbon bar can be worn alone on specified uniforms.

MARINE CORPS MARKSMANSHIP AND QUALIFICATION BADGES

THIS IS the largest section of this part because of two important factors. First, the Marine Corps puts a much heavier emphasis on marksmanship than any other branch of the military; second, the Marine Corps authorizes for wear upon the military uniform the badges and awards won by many of the winners of intra-service and inter-service trophies for shooting.

36. Distinguished Marksman Badge

This badge is awarded to all Marine Corps and Marine Corps Reserve personnel who have attained the status of Distinguished Marksman with the rifle in competitive matches. It is a shield-shaped plaque in gold. In the center is a white and black enameled target; above this is the word "Distinguished" and below it the word "Marksman." The shield is framed and is connected to a suspension bar by rings. The suspension bar in gold is framed, with small gold balls at the ends, and within the bar appears "U.S. Marine Corps" in raised letters. The reverse of the badge is blank, suitable for engraving the recipient's name.

37. Distinguished Pistol Shot Badge

This badge is slightly smaller than the Distinguished Marksman Badge, but is almost identical in appearance. It is awarded to all Marine Corps and Marine Corps Reserve personnel who have attained the status of distinguished pistol shots in competitive matches. It is a shield-shaped plaque in gold with a black and white enameled target in

36

37

38

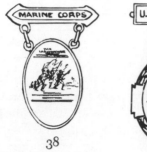

39

40

41

42

43

44

45

46

the center. Above this is the word "Distinguished," and below are the words "Pistol Shot." They frame the plaque, which is attached to a top suspension bar by rings. The bar is framed, with small gold balls at the ends, and appearing within the bar are the words "U.S. Marine Corps." The reverse is blank, suitable for engraving the recipient's name.

38. **Lauchheimer Trophy Badges**

These badges are awarded to competitors attaining the first, second, and third highest aggregate scores with both rifle and pistol in the annual Marine Corps competitions. The badges are in gold, silver, and bronze, and are awarded in that order for the highest scores in order of merit. The recipient of the gold badge is also awarded the Lauchheimer Trophy and a letter from the Commandant of the Corps. The award is presented in the name of the late Brigadier General Charles H. Lauchheimer, USMC, by his family. The badge is an oval-shaped plaque charged with a scene of a Marine detachment with colors flying, which appears between the words "The Lauchheimer Trophy for annual competition in small arms firing," at the top, and, at the bottom, "Presented to the United States Marine Corps by the family of Brig. Gen. Charles H. Lauchheimer." The badge is connected to a top suspension bar by rings. The bar is straight with tips like arrow points, and within this appear the words "Marine Corps." The reverse is plain, suitable for engraving the recipient's name.

39. **Marine Corps Rifle Championship Badge (McDougal Trophy)**

This badge is awarded to the highest scoring eligible competitor in the annual Marine Corps Rifle Competition. The David S. McDougal Memorial Trophy is also awarded with the badge. The trophy and badge were originated by the family and friends of the late Lieutenant Colonel David S. McDougal, USMC, a distinguished marksman, who gave his life for his country in World War II.

The badge, in gold, has a wreath-bordered disk charged with a figure of a prone Marine rifleman in firing position, behind a mounted scope. This is placed on a decorative cross, and above the figure are the words "McDougal Trophy," while at the bottom is a Marine Corps emblem. The reverse is blank, suitable for engraving. The disk is suspended from a framed bar with small gold balls at the ends, in which appear the words "U.S. Marine Corps."

40. Marine Corps Pistol Championship Badge

This badge is awarded to the highest scoring eligible competitor in the annual Marine Corps Pistol Competition. The Marine Corps Pistol Trophy is also awarded with it. The badge consists of a decorative plaque charged with the figure of a Marine with pistol in the firing position. At the base of the plaque, below the figure, is the Marine Corps emblem. The plaque is connected to a suspension bar by rings. The bar is straight with small gold balls at the ends, with the words "U.S. Marine Corps" within it. The complete badge is gold. The back of the plaque is blank, suitable for engraving the recipient's name and date of award.

41. Marine Corps Rifle Competition Badges

This badge is awarded to the twelve highest scoring non-distinguished enlisted competitors of the regular Marine Corps in the Annual Marine Corps Competition. Two gold, three silver, and seven bronze badges are awarded in that order for highest scores in order of merit. Additional badges of appropriate degree are awarded to officers of the regular Marine Corps and to officers and enlisted men of the Marine Corps Reserve under the same conditions.

The badge is a disk in the appropriate metal, charged with a black and white enameled target in front of crossed rifles, in front of and above a wreath of laurel leaves, joined at the bottom by a bow knot. The Marine Corps emblem appears at the top of the disk, which is suspended from a decorative suspension bar by a series of rings, and the reverse is plain, suitable for engraving. The bar has pointed ends with the words "Marine Corps" in raised letters.

42. Marine Corps Pistol Competition Badges

This badge is awarded to the eight highest scoring nondistinguished enlisted competitors of the Regular Marine Corps in the annual Marine Corps Pistol Competition. One gold, two silver, and five bronze badges are awarded in that order for highest scores in the order of merit. Awards to officers of the Regular Marine Corps and to enlisted men and officers of the Marine Corps Reserve are awarded in the same manner as the previous competition badge.

The badge is a disk in the appropriate metal, charged with a black and white enamel target, flanked by 45-caliber automatic pistols, above and in front of a wreath of laurel leaves, joined at the bottom by a bow knot. The Marine Corps emblem appears at the top of the disk. The disk is attached to a suspension bar by rings. The suspension bar is as in the previous badge. The reverse of the disk is blank, suitable for engraving.

43. Division Rifle Competition Badges

These badges are awarded to the first ten per cent of the highest scoring nondistinguished enlisted competitors of the regular Marine Corps in each of the Marine Corps annual Division Rifle Competitions. One-sixth of the badges awarded are gold, one-third are silver, and one-half are bronze; they are awarded in that proportion for highest scores in order of merit. Additional badges are awarded to officers of the regular Marine Corps and to officers and enlisted men of the Marine Corps Reserve in the same manner as the previous badges. The badge is identical to the Marine Corps Rifle Competition Badge, with the exception that the Marine Corps emblem at the top of the disk is replaced by the word "division." The reverse is blank, suitable for engraving the recipient's name.

44. Division Pistol Competition Badges

These badges are awarded to the first 10 per cent of the highest scoring nondistinguished enlisted competitors of the regular Marine Corps in each of the Marine Corps annual Division Rifle Competitions. One-sixth of the badges awarded are gold, one-third are silver, and one-half are bronze; they are awarded in that proportion for highest scores in order of merit. Additional badges are awarded to officers of the regular Marine Corps and to officers and enlisted men of the Marine Corps Reserve in the same manner as the previous badges. The badges are identical to the Marine Corps Pistol Competition badges, with the exception that the Marine Corps emblem at the top of the badge does not appear and the word "Division" appears at the bottom, between the target and the wreath.

45. Interdivision Rifle Team Match Badge

This badge, in gold, is awarded to each shooting member of the winning team in the Marine Corps annual Interdivision Rifle Team Match. The winning team is also awarded the Interdivision Rifle Team Match Trophy, which is dedicated to the memory of those Marines instrumental in the furtherance of rifle matches who gave their lives in World War II. The badge is a rectangular plaque charged with a scene of five riflemen in prone firing position in front of an observer with mounted scope. In the background two tents and a Marine Corps emblem appear at the bottom over a band of leaves, in simulated encirclement of the plaque. At the top is a flat area, on which is engraved the date of the award. This plaque hangs from a top suspension bar by rings. The top bar is framed, with small gold balls at the ends, and the words "U.S. Marine Corps" in raised letters are within. The back is blank and suitable for engraving the recipient's name.

46. Interdivision Pistol Team Match Badge

This badge, in gold, is awarded to each shooting member of the winning team in the Marine Corps annual Interdivision Pistol Team Match. The team is also awarded the Interdivision Pistol Team Match Trophy, which is dedicated to the memory of those Marines instrumental in the furtherance of pistol matches who gave their lives in World War II. This badge is a shield-shaped plaque charged with a scene of five Marines in the firing position on the pistol firing line. It has a very decorative border all around the plaque, and at the bottom is a Marine Corps emblem. The plaque is connected to a suspension bar by rings. The top bar is framed, with small gold balls at either end, and in raised letters within the bar are the words, "U.S. Marine Corps." The reverse is blank and suitable for engraving the recipient's name.

Pacific Trophy Match Badge

This badge, in gold, is awarded to each shooting member of the winning team in the Pacific Trophy Match, an annual Marine Corps pistol team competition. The winning team is also awarded the Pacific Trophy. The badge is identical to the Interdivision Pistol Team Match Badge, except that the top suspension reads "Pacific Trophy." (Not shown.)

Edson Trophy Match Badge

This badge, in gold, is awarded to each shooting member of the winning team in the Edson Trophy Match, an annual Marine Corps pistol competition. The winning team is also awarded the Edson Trophy. The badge is identical to the Interdivision Pistol Team Match Badge, except that the top suspension bar reads "Edson Trophy." (Not shown.)

Holcomb Trophy Match Badge

This badge, in gold, is awarded to each shooting member of the winning team in the Holcomb Trophy Match, and annual Marine Corps pistol competition. The winning team is also awarded the Holcomb Trophy. The badge is identical to the Interdivision Pistol Team Match Badge, except that the top suspension bar reads "Holcomb Trophy." (Not shown.)

Shively Trophy Match Badge

This badge, in gold, is awarded to each shooting member of the winning team in the Shively Trophy Match, an annual Marine Corps pistol competition. The winning team is also awarded the Shively Trophy. The badge is identical to the Interdivision Pistol Team Match Badge, except that the top suspension bar reads "Shively Trophy." (Not shown.)

47. Elliott Trophy Match Badge

This badge, in gold, is awarded to each shooting member of the winning team in the Elliott Trophy Match, an annual

Marine Corps Rifle Team Competition. The winning team is also awarded the Elliott Trophy. The badge consists of a plaque, with decorative edges, charged with figures of riflemen on the firing line. One figure is in the standing, or offhand, position, another is sitting with his rifle across his knees, and a third is sitting behind the shooters with a mounted scope, acting as observer. There are clouds in the background. The plaque is attached to a suspension bar by rings. The bar is a straight, framed type, with the words "Elliott Trophy" in raised letters within. The back of the plaque is blank and suitable for engraving the recipient's name.

San Diego Trophy Match Badge

This badge, in gold, is awarded to each shooting member of the winning team in the San Diego Trophy Match, an annual Marine Corps Rifle Team Competition. The winning team is also awarded the San Diego Trophy. The badge is identical to the Elliott Trophy Match Badge, except that the top suspension bar reads "San Diego Trophy." (Not shown.)

Wharton Trophy Match Badge

This badge, in gold, is awarded to each shooting member of the winning team in the Wharton Trophy Match, an annual Marine Corps Rifle Team Competition. The winning team is also awarded the Wharton Trophy. The badge is identical to the Elliott Trophy Match Badge, except that the top suspension bar reads "Wharton Trophy." (Not shown.)

Lloyd Trophy Match Badge

This badge, in gold, is awarded to each shooting member of the winning team in the Lloyd Trophy Match, an annual Marine Corps Rifle Team Competition. The winning team is also awarded the Lloyd Trophy. The badge is identical to the Elliott Trophy Match Badge, except that the top suspension bar reads "Lloyd Trophy." (Not shown.)

Smith Trophy Match Badge

This badge, in gold, is awarded to each shooting member of the winning team in the Smith Trophy Match, an annual Marine Corps Rifle Team Competition. The winning team is also awarded the Smith Trophy. The badge is identical to the Elliott Trophy Match Badge, except that the top suspension bar reads "Smith Trophy." (Not shown.)

48. **F.M.F. Combat Infantry Trophy**

These badges, in gold, silver, and bronze, are awarded annually to individual members of Marine rifle squads that compete in the Corps-wide rifle squad combat practice competition. Rifle squads are selected from each infantry regiment in the Fleet Marine Force (F.M.F.) and represent the parent unit in the competition finals at Marine Corps schools. The first-place squad is issued gold, the second, silver, and the third-place, bronze badges. The badge consists of a circular plaque, with the arms of a cross behind it; resting between the arms are the leaves of a wreath of laurel. The top arm of the cross has the letters "F.M.F." In the center section appears a scene of a combat Marine squad in action, with the squad leader using a walkie-talkie. All figures are in full combat gear. Above this are the words "Combat Infantry Trophy." The pendant hangs from a straight-type suspension bar decorated on the top and bottom and bearing the words "U.S. Marine Corps."

49. **Annual Rifle Squad Combat Practice Competition Badge**

These badges, in gold, silver, and bronze, are awarded in the same manner as the previous award, and also for an annual competition; however, this is not limited to Fleet Marine Force units. The badge consists of a shield-shaped pendant with a Marine in full combat gear, carrying a Browning automatic rifle in a charging position. There is a wreath of laurel at the top of the shield, with the words "Annual Rifle Squad" above the figure and the word "Competition" below it. The badge hangs from a suspension bar by rings. The bar is framed, with rounded ends, and has the words "U.S. Marine Corps" in raised letters within it.

50. **Expert Rifleman Badge (Obsolete)**

This badge was awarded to all Marines who qualified as expert with the service rifle over a prescribed rifle qualification course. The badge is in silver. It consists of two Spring-

47

48

49

51

50

52

53

54

55

56

57

58

59

60

field model 1903, 30-caliber service rifles crossed in front of a wreath of laurel leaves, joined at the bottom in a bow knot. The pendant is suspended from a bar with decorated ends, in which the words "Expert Rifleman" appear.

51. Sharpshooter Badge (Obsolete)

This badge, in silver, was awarded to Marines who qualified as sharpshooter with the service rifle over the prescribed qualification course. The badge consists of a Maltese cross with a target in the center, which is suspended by rings from a straight suspension bar with rounded ends. On the bar appears the word "Sharpshooter."

52. Rifle Marksman Badge (Obsolete)

This badge, in silver, was awarded to Marines who qualified as marksmen with the service rifle over the prescribed qualification course. The badge consists of a wide bar with rounded ends in which appears the word "Marksman," with a small target at either end.

53. Pistol Shot, First Class Badge (Obsolete)

This badge was used for a very short period just prior to World War I. It consists of a suspension bar in silver with fluted ends, with targets at either end. Within the bar appear the words "Pistol Shot First Class." The badge was authorized for all Marines who attained that status on prescribed courses.

54. Marine Corps Basic Badge

This badge, in silver, is awarded to all officers and enlisted men of the Marine Corps who qualify with any weapon for which the award of a qualification bar is authorized. The badge consists of a target with a Marine Corps emblem at the top, and is completely enclosed by a wreath of laurel leaves, which is joined at the bottom with a bow knot. The pendant is connected to a top suspension bar, which is straight with pointed edges, on which the words "U.S. Marine Corps" appear in raised letters. Between the top bar and pendant are hung the qualification bars, for which the piece was issued. The bars are straight, with raised letters and a pebbled background.

The bars are as follows: Ex-Auto-Rifle, SS-Auto-Rifle, Ex-Auto-Rifle-B, and SS-Auto-Rifle-B for automatic rifles; Ex-Rifle-B, MM-Rifle-B, and SS-Rifle-B for rifle; Ex-S.M.G. and SS-S.M.G. for sub-machine gun; Ex-Carbine and SS-Carbine for carbine; Ex-Pistol and SS-Pistol for pistol. The rifle awards are for the "B" course, and are for Marine Reserve personnel only.

55. Rifle Expert Badge

This badge, in silver, is awarded to Marines who qualify as expert with the service rifle over a prescribed rifle qualification course. The badge consists of two 30-caliber M-1 service rifles, with slings, in front of a wreath of laurel leaves, joined at the bottom with a bow-knot. The pendant is suspended from a bar with decorated ends, in which the words "Rifle Expert" appear.

56. Rifle Sharpshooter Badge

This badge, in silver, is identical to the earlier sharpshooter badge, namely, a Maltese cross, but in this case a Marine Corps emblem appears in the center. This is joined to the suspension bar by rings. The suspension bar is straight, with rounded ends, and within it appear the words "Rifle Sharpshooter" in raised letters.

57. Rifle Marksman Badge

This badge, in silver, is awarded to all Marines who qualify as marksman with the service rifle. It consists of a target, hung by a series of rings to a top suspension bar, which is straight with rounded ends. Within it appear the words "Rifle Marksman."

58. Pistol Expert Badge

This badge, in silver, like all the pistol awards, is slightly smaller in size than those awarded for rifle qualification. It consists of crossed 45-caliber automatic pistols, on a wreath of laurel leaves, joined at the bottom by a bow knot. This is connected to a top suspension bar by rings. The top bar is straight with rounded ends, with the words "Pistol Expert."

59. Pistol Sharpshooter Badge

This badge, in silver, is awarded to all Marines who qualify as sharpshooters with the service pistol over prescribed courses. The badge is identical to the Rifle Sharpshooter Badge, only it is slightly smaller. The top suspension bar has the words "Pistol Sharpshooter."

60. **Pistol Marksman Badge**

This badge, in silver, is awarded to all Marines who qualify as marksmen with the service pistol over prescribed courses. The badge, though slightly smaller, is identical to the Rifle Marksman Badge. The top suspension bar has the words "Pistol Marksman."

AIR FORCE RIFLE AND PISTOL MARKSMANSHIP BADGES

61. **Distinguished Rifleman Badge**

This badge is awarded to all personnel of the Air Force who have attained the status of distinguished rifleman in competitive matches. It is a shield-shaped plaque in gold. In the center is a black and white enameled target, and above this is the word "Distinguished," while below it is the word "Rifleman." The shield is framed, and is connected to a suspension bar by rings. The suspension bar is framed, with small gold balls at the ends, and within the bar appear "U.S. Air Force" in raised letters. The reverse is blank, suitable for engraving the recipient's name.

62. **Distinguished Pistol Shot Badge**

This badge, slightly smaller than the Distinguished Rifleman Badge, but almost identical in appearance, is awarded to all Air Force personnel who have attained the status of distinguished pistol shot in competitive matches. The badge is a shield-shaped plaque in gold with a black and white enameled target in the center. Above this is the word "Distinguished," and below it the words "Pistol Shot." With them the plaque is framed. This is attached to a top suspension bar by rings; the bar is framed, with small gold balls at the ends, and appearing within the bar are the words "U.S. Air Force." The reverse is blank.

63. **Excellence-in-Competition National Match Rifleman Badge**

These are awarded in gold, silver, and bronze to personnel of the Air Force for excellence with the rifle in national match competition. The badge consists of a circular disk, which has a line design. To the left is the emblem of the Air Force, and to the right, above center, is a target in enamel. Behind this is a service rifle, and around the edge there are stars, thirteen in all. The whole is enclosed in a wreath of laurel leaves. It is attached to a top suspension bar by rings. The bar is straight with small balls at the ends, and within it are the words "U.S. Air Force." The reverse is plain, suitable for engraving.

64. **Excellence-in-Competition National Match Pistol Shot Badge**

This badge, in gold, silver, or bronze, is awarded to Air Force personnel for excellence with the pistol in national matches. It consists of a circular disk which has a line design. To the left is the Air Force Seal, and to the right, just above center, is an enameled target, with a 45-caliber automatic pistol. Thirteen stars are around the edge, and the whole is encircled by a wreath of laurel behind it. It is attached to a suspension bar by rings. The bar is straight with small balls at the ends, and within the bar are the words "U.S. Air Force." The reverse is blank, suitable for engraving.

65. **Non-National Match, Excellence-in-Competition Rifleman Badge**

These badges are awarded in gold, silver, and bronze to Air Force personnel who have attained certain excellence in competitive matches, although not on a national scale. They are awarded to the shooter in classes corresponding to achievement, and they are identical to the previous National Match Badge, with the exception that there is no wreath on the outer edge of the disk.

66. **Non-National Match, Excellence-in-Competition Pistol Shot Badge**

These badges are awarded in gold, silver, and bronze to Air Force personnel who have attained certain excellence in competitive pistol matches, although not on a national scale. They are awarded to the shooters in classes corresponding to their performance. They are identical to the previous National Match Badge, except that there is no wreath on the outer edge of the disk.

COAST GUARD COMPETITION BADGES

Coast Guard Rifle Competition Badges

This badge is awarded in gold, silver, and bronze, and the design of all three badges is the same. It is a large shield, framed, and within this is the square target, enameled black and white, and set upon a wreath. This is in turn set upon crossed rifles, and above the target appears the word "Rifleman." The shield is suspended from a framed rectangular clasp, which has the words "U.S. Coast Guard" in raised letters. The badges are in gold, silver, or bronze to indicate the recipient's score and placement in competitive matches. (Not shown.)

67. **Coast Guard National Competition Rifle Badges**
These badges are identical to the above competition badges, with the addition of the word "National," which appears in the bottom of the shield in raised letters.

Miniature Distinguishing Marks

These small ¼-inch crossed rifles are worn upon the ribbon bar of the Coast Guard Expert Rifleman's Medal to signify that the recipient is entitled to the above badges. These crossed rifles are in the same metal as the badge awarded: gold, silver, or bronze. To indicate a national competitive shooter a small target in silver and black enamel is worn upon this ribbon. Miniature crossed carbines are also awarded. (Not shown.)

Coast Guard Pistol Competition Badge

This badge is awarded in gold, silver, and bronze, and the design of all three badges is the same. It is a large framed shield, in the center of which is another shield, enameled

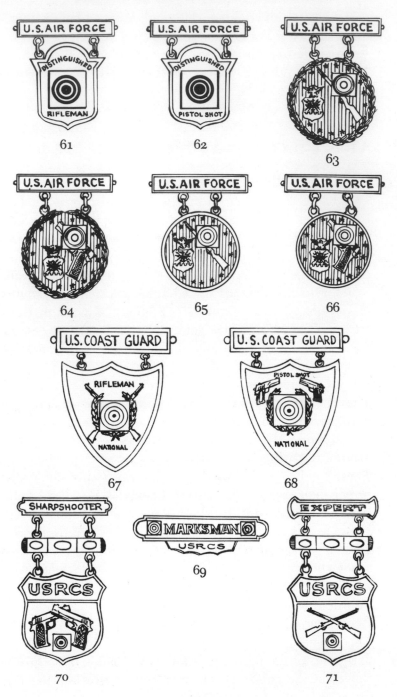

61

62

63

64

65

66

67

68

SHARPSHOOTER

69

71

70

black and white and superimposed upon a wreath of laurel leaves. At the top of the shield appear two 45-caliber automatic service pistols, to either side. Above these are the words "Pistol Shot." The shield is suspended from a framed rectangular pin bar by chain links. The bar has ball tips, and within it the words "U.S. Coast Guard" appear in raised letters. The badges are in gold, silver, or bronze to indicate the recipient's score and placement in competitive national matches. (Not shown.)

68. Coast Guard National Competition Pistol Badges
These badges are identical to the above competition badges, with the exception that the word "National" appears at the bottom of the shield. They are also awarded in gold, silver, and bronze.

Miniature Distinction Badges
These small ¼-inch crossed pistols in gold, silver, and bronze are worn upon the Coast Guard Expert Pistol Shot Medal ribbon bar. These crossed pistols are in the same metal as the badge awarded, namely, gold, silver, or bronze. If the marksman has won a National Competitive Badge, a small silver and black enameled target is worn on the ribbon.

REVENUE CUTTER SERVICE SHOOTING MEDALS

THE FOLLOWING BADGES were awarded to the men of the Revenue Cutter Service, who with the men of the Life-Saving Service were combined into a single organization, the United States Coast Guard, by Act of Congress, January 28, 1915. Note the similarity between the rifle and pistol badges, and between those of the present Coast Guard Pistol and Rifle Expert badges.

69. Revenue Cutter Service Marksman Badge
This bronze badge consists of a rectangular bar with decorative rounded edges. The whole is framed, and within this, at either end, are small raised targets. Within the bar is the

word "Marksman" in raised letters, and below this a small decorative plaque with the letters "USRCS" in raised letters. This badge is to distinguish the recipient as a qualified marksman with the rifle or with the pistol.

70. Revenue Cutter Service Expert or **Sharpshooter**

This is a shield-shaped pendant in bronze. The upper part has the letters "USRCS" in raised letters; the lower section has crossed 45-caliber automatic pistols, and below and between these is a raised target. The top bar is either the sharpshooter or expert pin already described. The pendant and pin are attached by a series of rings. Between the bar and pendant is worn a decorative bar of bronze with oval cutouts. These cutouts have a silver insert with the date of requalification engraved thereon.

The same badge is awarded to both experts and sharpshooters, the only difference being the bar at the top. The sharpshooter's top pin is a small rectangle with rounded ends and the word "Sharpshooter" is in raised letters. The expert's top pin is a framed rectangle with wide, flared, rounded edges, and the word "Expert" in raised letters.

71. Revenue Cutter Service Expert or **Sharpshooter**
Rifleman Badge

This badge is awarded for either expert or sharpshooter qualification by using either top pin, as previously described. The requalification bars previously described are also used. The medal pendant consists of a shield-shaped pendant of bronze. The upper part has the letters "USRCS" in raised letters. The lower part has crossed rifles, and below them is a target. The reverses of both of these badges are blank, suitable for engraving the recipient's name.

PART IV

Corps Badges and Shoulder Insignia

1

2

3

4

5

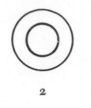

6

7

8

9

10

11

12

13

14

15

16

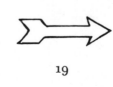

17

18

19

20

CIVIL WAR CORPS BADGES

Until the Civil War (1861–1865), units were usually distinguished by their uniforms. The great number of men in uniform during this war necessitated the use of a distinctive uniform for each of the opposing armies.

During the summer of 1862, one of the most popular officers of the Union, General Philip Kearny, mistook some officers for stragglers from his own command. General Kearny started to give them a dressing down, "emphasized by a few expletives," and the officers listened in silence until the General had finished. Then one of the officers saluted him and suggested that perhaps the General had made a mistake, for none of them belonged to his command. General Kearny, with his usual courtesy, exclaimed, "Pardon me! I will take steps to know how to recognize my own men hereafter."

The result was an order issued by Kearny that officers of his command should thereafter wear "on the front of their caps a round piece of red cloth to designate them." Thus was born the famed "Kearny patch." It is believed that General Kearny did not actually designate the shape of the patch, for at first almost any piece of red cloth was acceptable. General Kearny even donated his own red blanket to be cut up by his officers. Some covered their entire caps with red cloth. It is interesting to note that this same general, who took the first steps during the Civil War to decorate his men, brought about the adoption of both the "Kearny Crosses," which are illustrated in my book *American War Medals and Decorations*. This was one of his last wishes before he was killed in action.

Although Kearny had designated the patch to distinguish his officers from others, the enlisted men of his command very soon adopted it, often using pieces cut from the red linings of their overcoats. The men idolized Kearny and were anxious to identify themselves as members of his command. The patch is said to have reduced straggling — and even the Confederates are said to have given special attention to wounded and dead wearing the patch because they recognized the valor of Kearny's troops.

Quickly the idea spread to other divisions and corps. By March 1863 the first systematic plan for assigning corps badges to an entire army was adopted by the Army of the Potomac: a sphere for the First Corps, a trefoil for the Second, and so on.

By the end of the war almost all the corps had some sort of identifying insigne. Most of them were quite plain; however, some, such as that of the Fifteenth Corps, told quite a story. According to that story, in the fall of 1863 the Eleventh and Twelfth corps were sent to aid in the relief of Chattanooga. The eastern troops were much better dressed, and, in fact, corps badges were almost unknown in the western units. This caused some sharp words between the men. One day an enlisted man in General Logan's corps was asked where his corps patch was. Clapping his hand on his cartridge box, he said, "Forty rounds. Can you show me a better one?" Shortly thereafter, General Logan issued an order prescribing that the badge for the Fifteenth Corps should be a "miniature cartridge box and above the box will be inscribed the words 'Forty Rounds.'" Another patch that tells a story is that of the Fourteenth Corps, whose members often referred to themselves as "acorn boys" because at one time, when rations were scanty, the men roasted and ate acorns. In 1864, this corps chose an acorn as its distinctive patch.

In most instances these badges were adopted by a general order, often after some sort of competition for designs.

To a considerable extent the adoption of these corps badges was a morale-building factor, and often the enlisted men contributed materially to the designs. As a general rule, the divisions within each corps used a different color. The first division's patch would be red, the second's white, and the third's blue. When a corps had a fourth division, as was sometimes the case, another color would be designated.

Even after the war veterans cherished their badges, which were quite often seen in parades of the Grand Army of the Republic. Many of these badges were offered for sale to the troops during the war, and were widely advertised in newspapers. Many veterans had models of their badges made in enamel, silver, or gold, and wore them pinned to the breast or suspended from a ribbon around the neck during the parades and at meetings or encampments of the Grand Army of the Republic.

Although some people collect these badges, it is considered somewhat risky, because many of the originals were very crude, and, in fact, many of the shapes have been used for all types of organizations and are often seen as jewelry, stars, spheres, crosses, and the like.

In the descriptions of the following badges, none of the colors are dealt with; only the shapes used by the corps are described. In the case of those few corps that never officially adopted a badge, the badge that was chosen unofficially is described, or even those chosen by the veterans themselves after the close of the war.

As the use of these symbols developed amid the exigencies of the Civil War, it took on added significance as a practical tool of leadership. Through the use of these badges and by other means, such as flags and medals, military leaders were able to communicate a pride in organization to their men.

1, 2. First Corps
   A circle or sphere. Also shown as a circle within a circle, or a sphere without a center.
3. Second Corps
   A trefoil, or a shape commonly called a club.
4, 5. Third Corps
   A diamond shape. Also shown as a narrow diamond shape.
6. Fourth Corps
   A triangle with two equal sides, inside which is a smaller triangle. This corps never had an official badge, and the corps flag showed a square with an eagle, wings spread, at the center.

7. **Fifth Corps**

A cross pattée with very wide edges and very narrow center; this is quite often incorrectly called a Maltese cross.

8. **Sixth Corps**

A cross with arms of equal width, this badge was usually worn as a St. Andrew's cross, tilted like an "X."

9. **Seventh Corps**

An inverted crescent, the edges pointed down. Within the crescent is a five-pointed star, one point down. The badge is similar to the emblems of the Moslem world.

10. **Eighth Corps**

A six-pointed star, or two inverted overlapping triangles, like the Star of David.

11. **Ninth Corps**

A shield shape, and within this, a field cannon and an anchor crossed diagonally.

12. **Tenth Corps**

A diamond shape overlapping smaller diamond shapes at the points. It is similar to an outline of a fortress of the period. Within this shape is a flower of four points. This is an unofficial badge. Some members wore a square with a figure "10" within it.

13. **Eleventh Corps**

An increscent, or inverted crescent.

14. **Twelfth Corps**

A five-pointed star, one point up.

Thirteenth Corps

No badge was ever adopted or worn, officially or unofficially.

15. **Fourteenth Corps**

An acorn, or acorn outline.

16. **Fifteenth Corps**

A Civil War infantry cartridge box, with the words "forty rounds" above in a semicircle. This design sometimes appears within a diamond shape or a square.

17, 18. **Sixteenth Corps**

First, two crossed field cannons, crossed, muzzles up, within an outer circle.

Also, a circular cross pattée like a St. Andrew's cross with wide flared edges. This is a very decorative cross.

19. **Seventeenth Corps**

An arrow or arrow outline.

20. **Eighteenth Corps**

A decorative cross with rounded ends and points between the arms. Within the cross on the vertical arms appear triangles. This was an unofficial badge. Sometimes a square with the numeral "18" within was used.

21. **Nineteenth Corps**

A cross pattée, with the center arms joined in a circular design. This badge also appeared with the numeral "19" within the center design.

22. **Twentieth Corps**

A five-pointed star within another five-pointed star, with one point up. The inner star is cut out, or is in a color signifying the division.

23. **Twenty-First Corps**

This corps never had an official patch, but a design, which was in fact their corps flag, appeared sometime after the war. This was rectangular, separated into three horizontal sections, red at the top, white in the center, and blue at the bottom. Centered in the white is an American eagle with a shield at its front, and within the shield is the figure "21."

24. **Twenty-Second Corps**

A five-armed cross of unusual design, flared at the ends and narrow in the center of each arm.

25. **Twenty-Third Corps**

A shield, separated in the center into three quadrilateral, colored sections.

26. **Twenty-Fourth Corps**

A heart shape. It appeared as a heart with the figure "24" within.

27, 28. **Twenty-Fifth Corps**

A square, and centered within it, a diamond shape of equal size touching the edges.

21

22

23

24

25

26

27

25

28

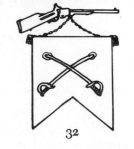

29

30

31

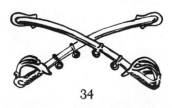

32

33

34

35

36

29. Sheridan's Cavalry Corps

This is a very decorative badge. It has an oval center, and within this is a pair of crossed cavalry sabers in their scabbards. The outer edge of the oval is beaded. Radiating from the oval is a sunburst pattern of thirty-two arms.

30. Engineer Corps Badge

During the war, this was called both the Engineer and the Pontonier Corps, hence the design of the badge, which has two decorative oars, crossed over a naval anchor, encircled at the top and sides by a scroll, and surmounted at the top by a castle. (The castle was adopted by the Army to signify engineers as early as 1840.)

31. Hancock's First Corps
(United States Veterans' Volunteer Corps)

Centered in a circle appears a portcullis, or gateway of a castle, in red with a yellow background. This is completely encircled by a wreath of laurel leaves, and radiating out from this wreath are seven designs, showing a hand holding a staff, with compass points at the ends. These are connected by fine lines curved at the ends.

32. Wilson's Cavalry Corps

This beautiful badge has a small Sharp's cavalry carbine, and suspended below this on a small chain is a cavalry guidon or flag, with points down, and decorative edges. The flag is red, and centered upon it are crossed cavalry sabers, cased in gold.

The following badges, although not in fact corps badges, were in use during the Civil War. They were forerunners of the service insignia later used.

33. Infantry

A rather large, curved decorated military bugle. This badge of brass was worn on the hat. The same insigne was carried out in thread, and later designs in brass showed a threaded design, but the decorations on the bugle had been removed.

34. Cavalry

Two crossed cavalry sabers in their sheaths, hilts down. The

Army of the Potomac used the Cavalry Badge, as shown, for its cavalry corps. However, the Army of the Cumberland and the Military Division of Mississippi used crossed cavalry sabers without the sheath.

35. **Signal Corps**

This badge, carried out in silver, shows crossed signal flags of the period. The one at the right had a blue rectangle in the center, the one at the left, a red star. Behind the flag is a signal torch in an upright position.

36. **Artillery**

This badge, adopted in 1836, had two Mexican War–style field cannons, crossed diagonally, and was carried out in brass.

SPANISH-AMERICAN WAR CORPS BADGES

DURING THE SPANISH-AMERICAN WAR (1898), the use of corps badges, which were first used during the Civil War, once again came into being. Many units, however, used only collar ornaments, such as "U.S. Vols." (U.S. Volunteers), for identification The war was so short that nothing more was needed, for very few men came into the service compared with the number during the Civil War.

The arm and service insignia, worn on the collar (dealt with in another section), were in use between the Civil War and World War I.

WORLD WAR I TO PRESENT: CORPS BADGES

AT THE TIME OF America's entry into World War I, the situation was similar to that of the Civil War. More and more men were coming to the colors, all wearing the same uniform, with only very small circular collar ornaments showing the branches of service. There was nothing whatsoever to show which state a man came from, or to which unit he belonged. Sooner or later the American spirit of individuality was sure to come forth.

In July 1918, the embarkation officer in charge of the Embarkation Center at Hoboken, New Jersey, noticed that the men of the newly arrived Eighty-first Division were wearing a distinctive insigne on the left arm of their trooper's uniform. The Eighty-first Division was composed of men from North and South Carolina and Florida. The men of this division chose to wear a "wildcat," representing an animal common to the mountains of the Carolinas, to signify the area they came from. The wildcat was of different colors, according to the different units within the division. The patch was made of cloth, with a wide outer circle in color. The inner circle was the uniform khaki cloth, and the wildcat was within this in the same color as the outer circle. The embarkation officer at Hoboken reported the matter to the War Department, and inquired whether permission existed for the wearing of such insignia. The War Department recognized that the idea of a "divisional insigne" was an excellent one, helping as it did in the identification and reassembling of units, which necessarily became mixed in the confusion of movements of large armies, and released an explanation of this report.

The Eighty-first Division was shipped to France in August 1918, still proudly wearing its unofficial patches. Upon their arrival in France, this distinguishable insigne again caused much comment and even orders for its removal. It was felt that no unit of the American Expeditionary Force had the right so to distinguish itself above all others. The matter came to the attention of General Headquarters, A.E.F., which upon investigation decided that the morale and temper of this division were worthy of emulation. The patch was recognized for its value as a means of building morale and of helping troops reassemble after an offensive.

Subsequently, all organizations of the American Expeditionary Force were directed to adopt similar insignia. This order, along with the report of the War Department, led to the present system of unit identity. The Eighty-first (Wildcat) Division must

be credited with originating this system of shoulder sleeve identification for the armed forces. Permission to wear such patches
was granted on October 19, 1918.

Many of the early patches were made in France, while the
divisions were in the field, and thus were often crude in appearance. Many were cut-out patches of felt, appliquéd on a background of the usual military uniform. Patches most recently
produced are embroidered. Very few of the original World War I
patches remain to this day, but for collectors of such material
many of the World War I patches have been made by current
manufacturers.

These brightly colored insignia, worn on the left sleeve
below the shoulder to denote divisions, corps, armies, or special
commands, resemble in appearance the enameled "corps badges"
of the Civil War and the Spanish-American War.

The terms "shoulder patches" and "divisional insignia" were
common during World War I and in fact are still in use; however
the official designation is "shoulder sleeve insignia."

This section has two parts. The first describes the patches in
use during World War I, and the second deals with patches of
World War II, the Korean War, and the present time. Many of
the patches of World War I were used again in World War II;
however, for clarity's sake, they are shown in both sections.

We will not attempt to deal with any of the squadron insignia as used in the Air Corps of the Army, the Air Force, or air
wings of the Navy and Marine Corps. This type of insigne was
often used on aircraft only, and thus was never part of the uniform. They are, at any rate, so numerous that it would be impossible to include them in this book.

37. **First Army**
   This is a large gothic "A " In the lower part of the letter
   appeared different arms of the service, a red and white
   patch for artillery; red castle for engineers; red, white, and
   blue cockade for the Air Service, etc.

38. **Second Army**
   A large gothic "2," the upper half red and the lower, white.

This comes from the Army Headquarters flag, which uses the same colors.

39. Third Army

This consists of a dark blue circle, within which is a red circle, representing an "O," and centered within the red circle is a gothic letter "A," in white. The "A" and "O" stand for Army of Occupation.

40. First Division

A large pointer shape of khaki; centered within this is a numeral "1" in red. The First is nicknamed the Big Red One.

41. Second Division

This design was carried out in a number of different shapes, pentagons, diamonds, circles, etc., to show the various regiments, and different colors to signify the battalion or company, but the center design was always the same: a five-pointed star in white, and within the star, the head of an Indian in full-dress war bonnet.

42. Third Division

A square, consisting of diagonal stripes of blue and white of equal widths, the blue at each edge. The three stripes of white stand for the division number, the blue for loyalty.

43. Fourth Division

Four ivy leaves representing the divisional number, on a khaki diamond. The pronunciation of "i-vy suggests the roman numeral "IV."

44. Fifth Division

A red diamond. The Fifth is known as the Red Diamond Division.

45. Sixth Division

A six-pointed star in red. The badge is often seen with a figure "6" superimposed in blue on the star, but this was never authorized.

46. Seventh Division

A circle of red, with an hourglass of black within. This was formed using two number "7s," one inverted and one upright.

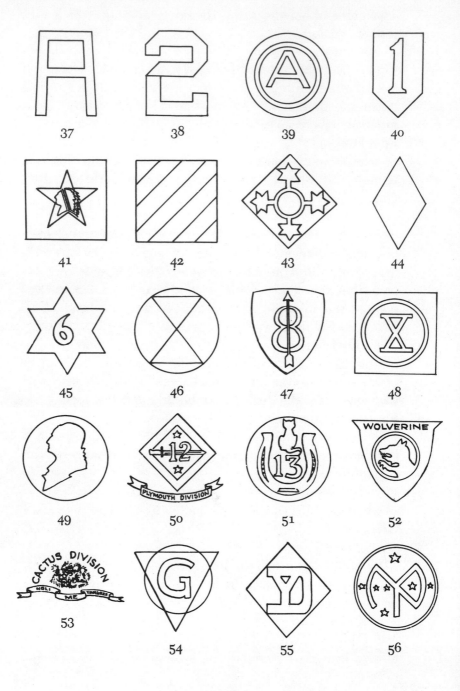

37   38   39   40

41   42   43   44

45   46   47   48

49   50   51   52

53   54   55   56

47. Eighth Division

A shield of blue, with the numeral "8" in white at the center. Through the numeral an arrow, in gold, points upward. The design is derived from the division name, "Pathfinder."

48. Tenth Division

A square of light blue, within this a circle of yellow and within the circle the Roman numeral "X" in yellow.

49. Eleventh Division

A red circle within which is a silhouette of the Revolutionary War hero Lafayette, in blue. The Eleventh was known as the Lafayette Division.

50. Twelfth Division

A blue diamond, with wide yellow edges; horizontally centered in the blue is a bayonet in yellow, and superimposed upon this, the numeral "12" in red. White five-pointed stars, above and below. At the bottom of this design is a scroll in blue, with the words "Plymouth Division" in white. That name was chosen for the division because it came from New England.

51. Thirteenth Division

This patch is a blue circle, with two proverbial bad luck symbols, the figure "13" in white, and a black cat, surrounded by a good luck horseshoe in red.

52. Fourteenth Division

A shield of green; in the center, a black circle and an outline of a wolverine in black, with a yellow background. Above this is the word "Wolverine" in yellow. This was chosen because the division was formed in Michigan, where the wolverine originates.

53. Eighteenth Division

This Division was known as the Cactus Division, and it developed a patch which has a cactus plant in green. Above this are the words "Cactus Division" in a semicircle, in green, and below it a scroll with the Latin motto *"Noli Me Tangere"* ("Touch Me Not").

54. Nineteenth Division

A triangle, point down, superimposed on a red circle, the

points extending beyond the edges of the circle. Where the points extend they are white, the inner section of the triangle is black, and within this the letter "G" is also white. This unit was established after 1918.

55. Twenty-sixth Division

This patch is a diamond shape in khaki, within which are the letters "YD," for Yankee Division, in blue gray, joined in a design.

56. Twenty-seventh Division

This patch is a black circle, with a red outer edge. Within the circle are a monogram insigne "N.Y." in red, and the seven stars of the constellation Orion, in reference to the World War I divisional commander, General J. F. O'Ryan. The stars are also in red. An unusual feature of this patch is that it was allowed to be worn only by "first-class troops."

57. Twenty-eighth Division

A red keystone, representing the state seal of Pennsylvania.

58. Twenty-ninth Division

Derived from the Korean symbol of good luck, the design of the patch is half blue and half gray, because the troops came from both North and South. It was called the Blue and Gray Division.

59. Thirtieth Division

Known as the Old Hickory Division, the Thirtieth Division had a patch that is a red oval with the outer edge in blue, representing the letter "O." Within it was a horizontal "H," with the Roman numeral "XXX" inside the cross bar of the "H," all in blue. This badge has always been worn horizontally, not vertically as the design reads.

60. Thirty-first Division

The Thirty-first was known as the Dixie Division, because it was formed in the South. Its patch is a white circle with a wide red border. Within it are two Ds in red, standing for "Dixie Division."

61. Thirty-second Division

The patch, a red arrow piercing a line, was selected because the Thirty-second "shot through every enemy line."

62. Thirty-third Division

A black circle, and a cross in yellow centered within it.

63. Thirty-fourth Division

This badge bears a black outline of an olla, a Mexican water flask. Within it is a bovine skull in red; above that is a numeral "34," and below it the words "sandstorm division," both in white. The elements of the badge symbolize New Mexico, where the division trained.

64. Thirty-fifth Division

A blue circle, with the Santa Fe cross in white. It represents the marking used on the trail. The Thirty-fifth was known as the Santa Fe Division.

65. Thirty-sixth Division

A khaki circle, representing an "O"; within this a blue-gray Indian arrowhead, and within the arrowhead, a khaki letter "T." The letters stand for Texas and Oklahoma, the states in which the division was formed.

66. Thirty-seventh Division

The Thirty-seventh was known as the "Buckeye Division," and its patch, adapted from the state flag of Ohio, is a red and white disk, red at the center, white at the edge.

67. Thirty-eighth Division

This is a spade-shaped shield separated vertically in red and blue; superimposed upon this are the letters "CY" in white, for the division's name, the Cyclone Division.

68. Thirty-ninth Division

This one is a dark blue circle, with a red outer edge; within it, the Greek letter delta, in white and dark blue, and within this a triangle composed of three inner triangles, of white, red, and light blue. The delta was used to signify the fact that the division was formed from personnel from the Mississippi River Delta. The three triangles stand for the three states in the Delta region, Louisiana, Mississippi, and Arkansas.

69. Fortieth Division

This division was formed in the western states and was known as the Sunshine Division. The patch was a dark blue square, with a sun of twelve rays in yellow in the center.

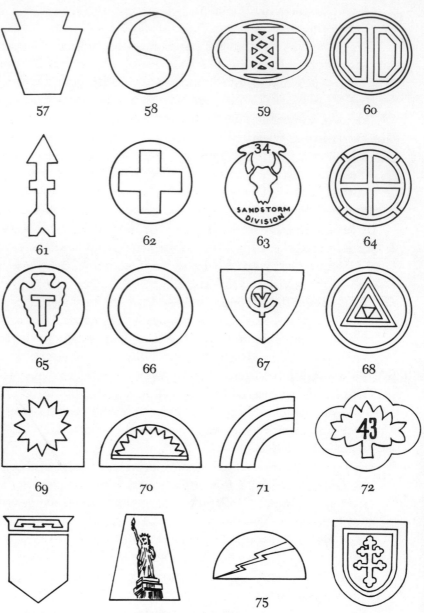

57

58

59

60

61

62

63

64

65

66

67

68

69

70

71

72

73

74

75

76

70. Forty-first Division

This patch consists of a half circle of khaki, and within this is a red sky, with a setting sun in yellow, over blue waters, signifying the Pacific. The patch was adopted to illustrate the divisional name, the Sunset Division.

71. Forty-second Division

The Forty-second was known as the Rainbow Division, because it was made up of troops from all over the United States. The patch chosen appropriately consisted of a rainbow pattern of red, yellow, and blue.

72. Forty-third Division

This patch is a red quatrefoil, representing the four New England states from which the division was formed after 1918. Within it is a black grape leaf, and within this is the figure "43" in gray.

73. Seventy-sixth Division

This is a shield shape of three parts. The upper part is blue and within this is a three-pronged label, or bar. The bottom shield shape is red and is separated from the top by a narrow white stripe.

74. Seventy-seventh Division

Known as the Liberty Division, this unit came from New York State. The patch is a light blue design, narrow at the top, wide at the bottom, and has centered within it the Statue of Liberty, in yellow.

75. Seventy-eighth Division

Originally this patch was a semicircle of red, used for the purpose of marking baggage. When shoulder insignia were adopted, a lightning bolt of white was added to the patch to represent the division's name, the Lightning Division.

76. Seventy-ninth Division

A shield shape, with the rounded bottom in dark blue, then a gray inner shape identical to the outside, and within this, dark blue again. Within this is the cross of Lorraine, French symbol of triumph since the fifteenth century. This emblem was chosen because the division was known as the Lorraine Division for its World War I service.

WORLD WAR I SHOULDER INSIGNIA

THE FOLLOWING SHOULDER PATCHES were quite unofficial during the World War I (1917–1918). But some, such as the First Marine Aviation Force insigne, may appear in photos or drawings of the period.

Most of these insignia were changed to the more accepted form shown on the previous pages. Then too, all these patches were made at the spur of the moment, often in the field, and though the general concept of the designs is shown, there remain many small variations of each design because of the "homemade" quality of their development. Thus they differ from the patches used during World War II (1941–1945), which were mass-produced to exacting standards on high-speed precision machines.

77. **Second Army**
A rather large gothic "B" in black (the First Army is signified by the letter "A"). In the open section of the bottom letter appears the device that tells in what unit within the Army the man served. In this illustration the device is that of headquarters, a blue square with an hourglass in white.

78. **Third Army**
A large gothic "C" in black, as used with the previous Army patches. In the illustration the individual's unit within the army appears in the open juncture of the "C." The center device is that of the Air Service, three circles of color known as a cockade; the outer circle is red, the center is white, and between these is a circle of blue.

79. **Third Army Aviation**
This patch was used upon aircraft and vehicles of the aforementioned unit and adopted later as a patch to be used in place of the letter "C." It is a cockade consisting of three circles, the outer one red, the next blue, and the center white; within the white center the numeral "3" appears in blue.

80. **First Marine Aviation Force**
This patch consists of a cockade of red, white, and blue, like

the previous patch, which was used on all aircraft of the United States during the war. Atop this cockade an American eagle with wings spread, in its beak and flowing above it a ribbon with the words *"Semper Fidelis"* ("Always Faithful"), the motto of the Marine Corps. Behind the cockade is the fouled anchor, which appears on all Marine Corps emblems. The device is almost the exact emblem used by the Marine Corps, except that the globe of the world is replaced by the cockade.

81. **Tenth Division**

This patch consists of a devil in either red or blue standing and holding a black pitchfork. The devil is usually outlined in white. This division did not reach France during World War I.

82. **Second Division**

One of the many patches used by the Second Division, A.E.F. It is a khaki circle with a wide outer edge in red. Centered within the khaki is a five-pointed star, one point down, in white, and upon this a silhouette in red of an American Indian in war bonnet.

83. **Sixth Division**

This was just one of many patches used by the "ready and traveling Sixth." This patch consists of a circular design with a cross at the top all in red; within this circular portion, centered, is a white disk.

84. **Fifteenth Division**

A coiled rattlesnake in white upon a khaki background. The division was called the Rattlesnakes.

85. **Thirty-ninth Division**

This patch has a wide circle of red, with a wide edge of white and an outer edge of black. The white and red were emblematic of the division name, for the Thirty-ninth was known as the Bull's-Eye Division.

86. **Seventy-eighth Division**

This patch was originally just a semicircle of red. The cloud area and three bolts of lightning, in white, were added when the division acquired the name Lightning Division.

87, 88. Eighty-ninth Division

This patch consists of stylized monograms in black, the letters are "M" and "W," and stand for the name of the division, the Middle West Division. This monogram was sewn upon a square of color that signified what regiment or company the man belonged to.

Another patch for the same division was a circle of light blue, with a wide outer circle of navy blue and the letter "M," also in navy blue, centered within the light blue center.

89. Ninety-first Division

A very large blue circle outlined with a wide band of white. Within the blue are the letters "WW," for "Wild West," where the division originated, and above this the numeral "91"; both of these are in white, matching the border.

90. Aviation Force or Corps

This is the patch that is usually worn within the army patch, as we have pointed out in describing the First, Second, and Third armies. It is a white center disk, with a dark blue circle enclosing it and at the edge another wide circle of red. This device was known as a cockade and was also painted on the sides and wings of aircraft.

91. 301st Tank Battalion

This was the first American tank force in France, and its patch was an inverted guidon, half yellow, to the left, and half red, to the right; it was worn points down. The yellow stands for cavalry and the red for artillery, as this movable (mechanized) artillery unit was a combination of the two services.

92. Trench Mortar Service

This patch consists of a rather large mortar bomb or shell. It was worn with the head down and fins up. The device is carried out in red, lightly outlined, with a dot pattern in white.

93. Eightieth Division

This very decorative patch has a shield in white with a

77

78

79

80

81

82

83

84

85

86

87

88

89

90

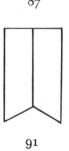

91

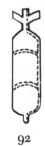

92

narrow outer border of blue. At the top of the shield is a sun with rays of red and white. Below this are three blue hills, representing the three states that furnished troops: Pennsylvania, West Virginia, and Virginia. The hills are blue because the division was called the Blue Ridge Division. Below this is the division's number, "80," and below the shield is a scroll with the words *"Vis Montium"* ("From the Mountains") in white on blue.

94. **Eighty-first Division**

A khaki circle, centered within which is the figure of a wildcat. At the outer edge is a wide border. The border and the cat are always the same color but this color varies with units within the division. This was the first patch ever worn and authorized for the Eighty-first.

95. **Eighty-second Division**

A red square; centered within it is a blue circle. In the blue circle are two stylized "As" which stand for "All American," the division's name. The "As" are in white or gold.

96. **Eighty-third Division**

This patch is a black inverted triangle, point down, with the letters of the word "Ohio" in a stylized monogram in gold. The division trained in Ohio.

97. **Eighty-fourth Division**

This was known as the "Lincoln Division"; its patch consisted of a white circle with a wide red border. Centered in the circle is an ax with red head and a blue handle. Above the ax is the word "Lincoln" and below it is the numeral "84," both in blue.

98. **Eighty-fifth Division**

A khaki circle, bearing the initials "C.D." in red, in honor of the divisional name, "Custer Division," so named for General George Armstrong Custer and for the camp where the division trained.

99. **Eighty-sixth Division**

A red shield, with a black hawk within. On the breast of the hawk is a smaller red shield with the letters "B.H." in black. The division was known as the Black Hawk Division.

100. Eighty-seventh Division

A green circle, with an acorn in khaki in the center. This stands for strength and signifies the divisional name, Acorn Division.

101. Eighty-eighth Division

This patch shows two figure 8s at the right angles, which form a clover leaf, representing the four states from which the division personnel were recruited. It is light blue, red, or black, according to what unit wore it.

102. Eighty-ninth Division

This division was known as the "Middle West Division." Its emblem is a khaki circle, with a wide black outer edge. Connected to this is the letter "W" in black. When inverted it becomes an "M," standing for the division name. The bottom was colored according to what unit wore it.

103. Ninetieth Division

A red monogram, consisting of the letters "T" and "O," the initials of Texas and Oklahoma, where the division was formed.

104. Ninety-first Division

The division was formed in the Far West and adopted the representation of the fir tree as typifying the area. An evergreen, it represents the readiness of the division. The tree is green.

105. Ninety-second Division

This patch is a khaki circle with a wide outer edge of black; within the circle is the silhouette of a buffalo. In World War I, the division was composed of Negro troops. They adopted this patch because many of the senior noncommissioned officers served on the frontier, where the Indians called Negro soldiers buffaloes.

106. Ninety-third Division

This patch is sometimes said to be the first patch used by the Ninety-third, but, in fact, it was used only by the 371st Regiment of the Ninety-third Division. It is a khaki patch, with a wide outer edge of red. Within the khaki circle is a red hand. This patch was granted to the 371st by the French

93

94

95

96

97

98

99

100

101

102

103

104

105

106

107

108

109

110

111

112

command for action at Verdun, in honor of the Regiment's work with a French Colonial unit which used this patch. It was known as the bloody hand.

107. Ninety-third Division

A black circle, with a French Army helmet in blue within it. This was symbolic of the Division's service with the French in World War I.

108. Ninety-fourth Division

This patch has a black silhouette of a Puritan with a blunderbuss on a circle of light gray.

109. Ninety-fifth Division

This patch was adopted after World War I. The red letters "O" and "K" are interlocking on a background of khaki. These letters stand for Oklahoma and Kansas, where the division was formed.

110. 101st Division

This patch was adopted after World War I. It consists of a black shield which stands for the "Iron Brigade" of Civil War fame, one regiment of which had had a famous war eagle, "Old Abe," which always screamed going into battle. The shield bears the head of a screaming eagle in white, with outspread wings in yellow below.

111. First Corps

This patch consists of three circles. The inner circle is black, the middle is white, and the outer circle is again black.

112. Second Corps

This is a blue rectangle with rounded ends, with an inner frame of white. Within this is the Roman numeral "II," standing for the corps number. At the left of this is the American eagle in white, and at the right is the British lion in white. This was symbolic of the Second Corps service with the British during World War I.

113. Third Corps

This patch represents a caltrap, an old military instrument with four sides. To impede the progress of enemy cavalry, it was placed on the ground so that, with any of three points on the ground, one would always project upward. The three outer angles are blue; the inner triangle is white. It is symbolic of the four divisions of the corps.

114. Fourth Corps
A circle separated into quarters. The right and left quarter sections are blue; the top and bottom ones are white.

115. Fifth Corps
A pentagon shape. The outer edges and dividing areas are khaki, and the inner triangles are white.

116. Sixth Corps
A circle of dark blue, with an inner border of dashes; centered within this border is numeral "6," and both are in white.

117. Seventh Corps
An unusual shape with six points in dark blue, and an inner border of dashes in white. Centered within this is the numeral "7" in white.

118. Eighth Corps
An octagon of blue, and within this is an octagonal border of white. Within the white is an octagonal border of blue, and centered within this is a figure "8," composed of two overlapping white octagonals with blue centers.

119. Ninth Corps
A blue circle; within this is a wide red circular border. Connected to this is the Roman numeral "IX" in red.

120. Second Corps School
Schools were organized in the various corps after the close of the fighting. The insignia were the same for all; only the numerals varied. The design was a white circle with a wide red outer edge. Within this is a large numeral ("2" in this case), at the left is the letter "C," and at the right, an "S," all in blue.

121. Third Corps School
The same design as above (120), but with the figure "3."

122. Ambulance Service
A red circle, and within it the well-known Gallic rooster in white. This is symbolic of the several ambulance companies of Americans in the French Army prior to America's entry into World War I.

123. Advance Section, Service of Supply

A circle of light gray with an outer border of blue. Within this is the Lorraine cross, and at the bottom at either side are the letters "A" and "S," both in red, for "advance section."

124. Tank Corps

A triangle divided into three sections, yellow at the top, and red and blue at the bottom. This is indicative of the fact that tanks combine the functions of cavalry, artillery, and infantry, for these are the colors of the three branches.

125. District of Paris

This patch is a triangle of dark blue, with one point down. Centered in this is a gray fleur-de-lis of the Bourbon kings.

126. Liaison Service

This insigne was adapted from the French General Staff insigne, with some minor changes. It is an unusual shape of dark blue; centered in this is a winged staff, with a fleur-de-lis at the top. At the bottom, issuing from the staff, are lightning bolts in white or yellow.

127. Postal Express Service

This is a rectangle of dark blue, within which is a greyhound running at full speed, in silver. Adopted for the couriers, it had its origin in the small silver greyhound carried by messengers of the king of England, who performed the same services and for whom it opened special doors when they desired quick transportation.

128. Army Artillery School

This patch was never approved by headquarters. It is a black circle, with a narrow outer edge in red. Within it is the head of Minerva, goddess of war, with a gold helmet and red plume.

129. North Russia Expedition

A light blue rectangle with a rounded top. Within this is a polar bear on an ice floe, both in silver.

130. Siberian A.E.F.

An artillery-shell shape in white, bordered by dark blue. In the center is a bear on its haunches in dark blue. The letter "S" in white for Siberia is superimposed in front of it.

113

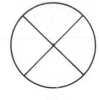
114

115

116

117

118

119

120

121

122

123

124

125

126

127

128

129

130

131

132

131. Camp Pontanezen

This patch was used for the camp at Brest, France, which was a center of incoming traffic in World War I. The patch is a red circle, and within this is a series of "duckboards" in white. These were the boards ordered by General Smedley Butler, U.S.M.C., to combat the mud.

132. Railway Artillery Reserve

This is a hexagon of light gray, with a red outer edge. Within the hexagon is a mythical bird in green, standing on a section of rail, with the letters "RAR" on it. Above the bird is a curved section of track almost encircling the bird.

133. Reserve Mallet

This patch is a green shield, and within it is a French infantry bugle in yellow. This unit was composed of Americans who went to France before the United States entered the war. After the American entry they stayed in the French service, constituting the reserve. They were called the Reserve Mallet, for their commanding officer, Captain Mallet of the French Army.

134. Thirteenth Engineers

This patch is a square in dark blue, and in a circle within the square are thirteen white stars, for the number of the unit. Within the stars is a castle in red. This is the emblem of engineers, but in this case the castle is thought to signify Verdun, where the unit served as a heavy railroad regiment.

135. Chemical Warfare Service

A shield, divided diagonally, with cobalt blue at the top and yellow at the bottom. These are the colors of the Chemical Corps.

136. Central Records Office

A shield in black, and within it a shield of red, white, and blue, with a lighter blue top. In that area are three five-pointed white stars. The whole is surmounted by an American eagle with wings spread, facing right.

137. Service of Supply

This insignia is a navy blue patch with rounded top. The

133

134

135

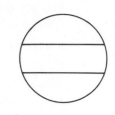

136

137

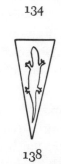

138

139

140

141

142

143

144

145

initials "SS," in monogram, centered, and in red, are for Service of Supply.

138. **Camouflage Corps**

An inverted black triangle, with a chameleon in yellow. This was appropriately adopted as the insigne for the Camouflage Corps.

139. **Railheads or Regulating Stations**

A black diamond, with a wide yellow outer edge. Within the black diamond is a gothic "R" in white.

140. **General Headquarters**

This patch was selected by General Pershing himself, at GHQ, Chaumont, France. It is a horizontally striped red, white, and blue disk.

The following three patches were adopted after the close of the war and were never officially authorized.

141. **Nineteenth Division**

A circle, with a large five-pointed star in the upper right, and below this, a half moon.

142. **Seventy-sixth Division**

A square, with the cracked Liberty Bell inside.

143. **Eighty-ninth Division**

A circle, with an eight-pointed star inside. In the center of the star is another circle.

Another type of unusual and different insigne came into use during World War 1 — the fighter pilot's squadron insigne. Most of the squadrons had badges made of metal and enamel. These badges were worn on the right uniform pocket, and some of them were made of silver or gold. Only two of these badges are illustrated because they are the only two that the author has seen.

144. **Ninety-fourth Fighter**

The famous "hat in the ring" — Uncle Sam's hat, with a blue crown and white stars and a hat band of white and red stripes, tilted through a red oval ring. This was carried out in enamel.

145. 147th Fighter

A standing Scots terrier. This badge was worn by then Lieutenant Charles D. Porter, a World War I ace.

WORLD WAR II SHOULDER INSIGNIA

THE FOLLOWING PATCHES came into existence just prior to World War II (1941–1945), during the war, and since. Many of the patches shown are no longer used; however, they are included as a guide. World War II saw the armed forces at the greatest strength in their history, so, most naturally, more patches were in use during this period than at any other time in our history. Though many of the patches of World War I were continued into the second war, they are shown again in their proper historical order.

146. First Army

A black gothic letter "A," with a khaki background.

147. Second Army

A gothic numeral "2," equally divided into two parts. The top is red, and the bottom white, on a khaki background.

148. Third Army

A blue circle, with an inner circle of red, representing an "O," and within this the letter "A" in white.

149. Fourth Army

A red diamond, within which is a four-leaf clover in white.

150, 151. Fifth Army

This is the original style but later was discontinued. It is a white pentagon with five five-pointed stars in red within it.

The second style consists of a red outer shape, and within it is a mosque in blue; within the mosque are the letter "A" and the numeral "5" in white.

152, 153. Sixth Army

The original insigne is a red hexagon, with a six-pointed star in white in the center.

The second style is a six-pointed white star, with a red inner border, and white at the edges. Within this is the letter "A" in red on a circular khaki disk.

154. Seventh Army

A blue triangle, and within it a pyramidal figure symbolic of the letter "A," with seven steps for the army number. The outer area is yellow and the inner area is red.

155. Eighth Army

A red octagon; the cross effect within is in white. It almost separates the area into four white and four red sections.

156. Ninth Army

This nine-sided shape is in red and is symbolic of the army number. Within this is an outline of a clover in white and within that is the letter "A" also in white.

157. Tenth Army

Two red triangles, one upright, one inverted, with points touching. The inner areas are white. The design represents the Roman numeral "X."

158. Fourteenth Army

An acorn shape in red, symbolizing strength. Within this is a decorative letter "A" in white.

159. Fifteenth Army

This is a pentagon shape, with an "A" in the center of it. The whole is divided by an "X" shape into both white and red. The five sides and the "X" for the Roman numeral together stand for the army number, fifteen.

160. First Corps

A black disk, with a wide white outer circle, and a narrow black border at the very edge.

161. Second Corps

This is a blue rectangle with rounded ends. Within this is a thin white frame, and centered within this is the Roman numeral "II," for the corps number. At the left of this is an American eagle, and at the right is a British lion, all in white.

162. Third Corps

This is a blue caltrap, of which the inner point is an inverted white triangle.

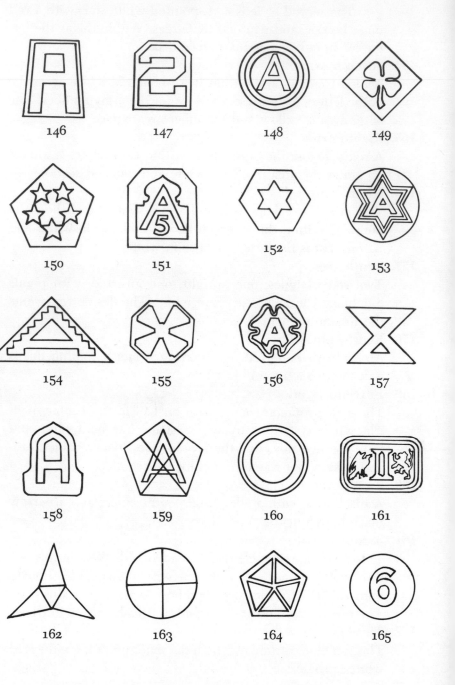

146   147   148   149

150   151   152   153

154   155   156   157

158   159   160   161

162   163   164   165

163. Fourth Corps

A circle, divided into quarter sections of white and blue.

164. Fifth Corps

A white pentagon, with white dividing lines, has five inner triangles of blue for the corps number.

165. Sixth Corps

A blue disk, with a white numeral "6" within it.

166, 167. Seventh Corps

A dark blue irregular shape, with the numeral "7" in white.

Alternately, a seven-pointed star in red, with the Roman numeral VII. The top half is blue and the bottom white, with the whole on a khaki disk.

168. Eighth Corps

A blue octagon, with an inner white frame. Centered within this is the figure "8," composed of two octagons, in white.

169. Ninth Corps

A blue disk, with a red inner circular frame; within this is the Roman numeral IX in red.

170. Tenth Corps

A disk, with the Roman numeral X within it. The disk is divided into blue and white. For the upper half, the top of the numeral is in white and the background is blue; for the lower half, it is just the opposite.

171, 172. Eleventh Corps

The first design became obsolete during World War II. It is a blue shield, and the upper lefthand corner is white with a red cross in it. In the lefthand corner of the cross is a green fir tree.

The second design is a blue disk with white dice, their red dots numbering eleven — five above and six below.

173. Twelfth Corps

The blades of a windmill superimposed on a shield of the City of New Amsterdam (an old name for New York). The shield is blue and the blades of the windmill are orange, the Dutch colors.

174. Thirteenth Corps

A green cloverleaf, suggestive of a figure "X," has superim-

166

167

168

169

170

171

172

173

174

175

176

177

178

179

180

181

182

183

184

185

posed upon it a red triangle, representing a three. This together is for the corps number, "13." The whole on a khaki disk.

175. Fourteenth Corps

A shield of Confederate gray, with a dark blue saltier; superimposed on this is a red caltrap. The four points of the caltrap plus the ten signify the Corps number, 14.

176. Fifteenth Corps

A khaki disk, with a blue outer edge, and within that the Roman numeral "X" in blue. Behind and below it is the numeral "V" (for five) in white. This is for the Corps number.

177. Sixteenth Corps

This large khaki shield has a narrow blue edge. Within this is a white compass rose with a blue center.

178. Eighteenth Corps

A white diamond shape with a blue edge, with silhouette of a dragon's head, also in blue.

179, 180. Nineteenth Corps

The first design became obsolete during World War II. It consisted of a red bell shape with a wide yellow border.

The newer design is a blue disk, with a white Indian tomahawk within, and a white border.

181. Twentieth Corps

A shield of blue with an outer border of yellow, and red at the edge. Within the blue shield are two crossed crampons in yellow, representing the Roman numeral XX, for the corps number.

182. Twenty-first Corps

A four-leaf clover in blue, centered within which is an acorn in red with crossed arrows. It is framed in white, and on a khaki background.

183. Twenty-second Corps

An arrowhead or pheon in blue and white.

184. Twenty-third Corps

An oval divided in two, with three crossed arrows, for the corps number. The top half is blue with white arrows, and the bottom is the reverse.

185. **Twenty-fourth Corps**

A blue shield with a white heart within. The heart has an inner frame of blue.

186. **Thirty-first Corps**

A six-sided blue shape, with three disconnected arms of a Maltese cross, in white.

187. **Thirty-third Corps**

A pentagon outline, with arrow points projecting from the angles. The design is divided vertically into blue and white. On the left, the angle outline and pointers are in blue over white; on the right, it is the reverse.

188. **Thirty-sixth Corps**

A trefoil, in blue. Within this are two interlocking triangles, divided into red and white.

189. **Fifteenth Army Group**

A red square, with a white and blue shield within it. The shield is composed of four white and four blue wavy lines.

The following patches are for Service Commands and were developed during World War II. All insignia are in blue and white, and the shape always signifies the service area number.

190. **First Service Command**

A white diamond with blue edges and a blue numeral "1" in the center.

191. **Second Service Command**

A blue square, with two interlocking squares of white.

192. **Third Service Command**

A three-pointed shield shape in white, with a wide blue edge. Within this is a three-pointed shape in blue.

193. **Fourth Service Command**

A blue disk, with a four-armed design within it, in white, has a blue design slightly tilted in the center.

194. **Fifth Service Command**

A blue disk, with a five-pointed design in white centered within. The center area is also blue.

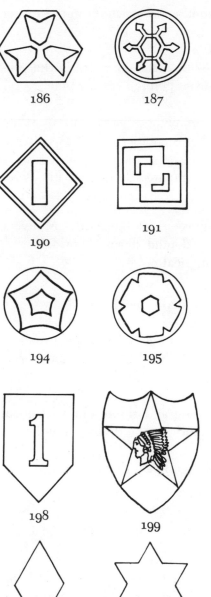

186

187

188

189

190

191

192

193

194

195

196

197

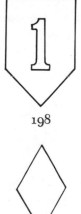

198

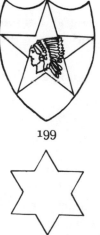

199

200

201

202

203

204

205

195. Sixth Service Command

A blue disk, with a six-pointed cross in white; in the center is a hexagon in blue.

196. Seventh Service Command

A blue disk, with a seven-pointed star in white in the center, has within it another seven-pointed star in blue.

197. Eighth Service Command

This is a blue disk, with an eight-pointed star in white within, in the center of which is another blue disk.

Ninth Service Command

This is a blue disk with a nine-pointed design in white, with a blue center. (Not shown.)

The following are for all the divisions of the Army. Many of them are the same as originally adopted during World War I, but they are again shown in numerical order.

198. First Division

A large red numeral "1" on a khaki shield.

199. Second Division

A very large black shield, with a five-pointed star in white. In the center of the star is the head of an Indian in war bonnet.

200. Third Division

A square comprising four blue and three white diagonal stripes. The white stripes stand for the division number.

201. Fourth Division

Four leaves of ivy in green on a khaki diamond shape.

202. Fifth Division

A red diamond shape.

203. Sixth Division

A six-pointed star in red.

204. Sixth Airborne Division

A shield, blue at the bottom for the sky, and with the top and lines in white to signify an open parachute. Above is a black curved design with the word "Airborne" in yellow.

205. Seventh Division

A red disk, with a black hourglass design in the center.

206. Eighth Division

A blue shield, with a white figure "8" centered in it. Behind this is an arrow in gold, pointing upward.

207. Ninth Division

A four-petal flower or double quatrefoil, divided in half. It is red at the top, blue at the bottom, and has a white center circle, all on a disk of khaki.

208. Ninth Airborne Division

Nine connected clouds of white, with a blue center. Within the center is a lightning flash in yellow. The Airborne tab above is black with yellow letters.

209. Tenth Mountain Division

This is in the shape of a blue powder keg with crossed bayonets of red in front, all outlined in white. Above this is a blue tab with the word "Mountain" in white. The same patch, without the "mountain" tab, was used by the original Tenth Light Division.

210. Eleventh Division

A disk, separated into twelve sections to resemble a clock. The sections are alternately blue and white, except that the top section, the area which represents twelve o'clock, is black.

211. Eleventh Airborne Division

A blue shield; centered within it is a winged circle in white with a red center, and the numeral "11" in white within it. The Airborne tab above is in blue with white letters.

212. Thirteenth Airborne Division

A blue shield, with a golden winged unicorn centered within. The airborne tab above is black with gold letters.

213. Fourteenth Division

A blue square with cut corners; within is a yellow St. Andrew's cross.

214. Seventeenth Division

A septfoil, or seven-lobed figure, with a white St. Andrew's cross within. The top and bottom areas of the background are blue, with the sides in red.

206

207

208

209

210

211

212

213

214

215

216

217

218

219

220

221

222

223

224

225

215. Seventeenth Airborne Division

A black disk, with the talon of an eagle in gold. The airborne tab above is in black with gold letters.

216. Eighteenth Airborne Division

This shield, with a blue sky and white clouds at the top, has a battle ax in yellow coming out from the clouds. The airborne tab above it is black with yellow letters.

217. Twenty-First Airborne Division

This blue disk, with white clouds at the top and center, has lightning bolts in yellow, coming from the clouds. The tab above is black with yellow letters.

218. Twenty-second Division

A red disk with a scorpion in gold on it.

219. Twenty-fourth Division

A red disk with a wide black border, and within it a taro leaf in green bordered in yellow.

220. Twenty-fifth division

A red taro leaf with yellow border; within it a lightning bolt in yellow.

221. Twenty-sixth Division

A khaki diamond, with a monogram "YD" in Blue.

222. Twenty-seventh Division

A black disk, with a red inner border, has a monogram "NY" and seven stars, as in the constellation of Orion. Both are in red.

223. Twenty-eighth Division

A keystone shape, for Pennsylvania, in red.

224. Twenty-ninth Division

The Korean symbol for luck, half blue and half gray.

225. Thirtieth Division

A red oval, with "O" and "H" in blue. Within the crossbar are three "Xs," also in blue, for the division's number.

226. Thirty-first Division

A white disk with a red inner border, and two Ds, one backward and one forward, in red.

227. Thirty-second Division

An arrow crossing through a line, all in red.

228. Thirty-third Division

A black disk, with a yellow cross centered on it.

229. Thirty-fourth Division

A black olla, or Mexican water flask, with a red bovine skull on it.

230. Thirty-fifth Division

A blue disk with a Santa Fe cross in white.

231. Thirty-sixth Division

A blue-gray flint arrowhead, with the letter "T" in khaki within, is also bordered in khaki.

232. Thirty-seventh Division

A white disk with a large red disk at its center.

233. Thirty-eighth Division

A spade-shaped shield, half red and half blue, with the red at the left. Centered on this is a monogram "CY" in white.

234. Thirty-ninth Division

A gray square with a rounded top. Within this is a white triangle framed in red; centered in the white is the letter "D," in blue.

235. Fortieth Division

A dark blue diamond shape, with a sunburst of twelve points in yellow centered on it.

236. Forty-first Division

A half circle bearing a yellow sunset with a red sky as background and a blue line at the bottom representing the Pacific Ocean.

237. Forty-second Division

A rainbow shape, red at the top, yellow in the center, and blue at the bottom.

238. Forty-third Division

A red quatrefoil with a black grape leaf centered on it.

239. Forty-fourth Division

An orange disk, with a wide blue border. Centered within is a monogram showing back-to-back figure "4"s in blue, forming a spearhead.

240. Forty-fifth Division

A red diamond shape with a thunderbird in yellow.

The division had adopted a design that consisted of a red square with a yellow swastika upon it, but that was discontinued in 1924.

241. Forty-sixth Division

A blue six-pointed star with a diamond in yellow at the back, all on a disk of khaki.

242. Forty-eighth Division

A stylized form of a cross in blue on white, with four areas of white and eight arms on the cross, an allusion to the division number.

243. Fiftieth Division

A red pentagon with a yellow border; within it is the figure "0" in yellow. Together the five-sided figure and the "0" stand for the division number.

244. Fifty-fifth Division

A blue pentagon with a yellow border; within it is the outline of another pentagon in yellow.

245. Fifty-ninth Division

A disk comprising a rattlesnake, coiled, in white, on yellow ground below, and dark blue in the background.

246. Sixty-third Division

This teardrop shape in khaki has within it flames in red, and superimposed on this is a sword in yellow, with a drop of blood on the blade.

247. Sixty-fifth Division

A blue shield with a halberd in white upon it.

248. Sixty-sixth Division

This yellow disk, with a narrow red border, has within it the head of a snarling black panther.

249. Sixty-ninth Division

A white square with a stylized figure conveying the impression of the figure "69" — the six in red, the nine in blue.

250. Seventieth Division

The over-all shape of an axhead in red; within it at the top

226

227

ABN

228

229

230

231

232

233

234

235

236

237

238

239

240

241

242

243

244

245

an axhead and -handle in white, and at the bottom a fir tree and grass in green with a white mountain peak in the distance.

251. Seventy-first Division

A white disk with a red border and the numerals "71" in dark blue.

252. Seventy-fifth Division

A shield, separated diagonally into equal parts of red, white, and blue, with the figures "7" in blue and "5" in red.

253. Seventy-sixth Division

An eared shield with a blue chief, which has a three-pronged label in white, and a bottom of red.

254. Seventy-seventh Division

A light blue shape, with the Statue of Liberty in yellow.

255. Seventy-eighth Division

A half circle in red, with a white streak of lightning diagonally across it.

256. Seventy-ninth Division

A dark blue shield, with an inner shield outline of blue-white, and within that a cross of Lorraine, also in blue-white.

257. Eightieth Division

An eared shield of khaki with a white border and white line near the bottom. Within this are three mountain peaks of light blue.

258. Eighty-first Division

A khaki disk with a wide black border; within it the figure of a wildcat in black.

259. Eighty-second Airborne Division

A red square; within it a blue circle. In the circle are the letters "AA" in white monogram form. The airborne tab is blue with white letters.

260. Eighty-third Division

A black inverted triangle with a cipher spelling out "Ohio" in yellow at the top center.

261. Eighty-fourth Division

A red disk has an ax and a split rail, both in white.

262. **Eighty-fifth Division**
A khaki disk with the letters "CD" in red, for Custer Division.

263. **Eighty-sixth Division**
A red shield, with a black hawk centered within. On the hawk is a red shield bearing the initials "BH" in black.

264. **Eighty-seventh Division**
A green disk with a yellow acorn centered on it.

265. **Eighty-eighth Division**
A four-leaf clover design of dark blue.

266. **Eighty-ninth Division**
A black letter "W" within a black letter "O," on a khaki background.

267. **Ninetieth Division**
A monogram combining the letters "T" and "O" in red, on a khaki background in a square shape.

268. **Ninety-first Division**
A green fir tree.

269. **Ninety-second Division**
A khaki disk with a wide black border, within which is the shape of a buffalo, also in black.

270. **Ninety-third Division**
A French helmet in light blue on a black disk.

271. **Ninety-fourth Division**
This is a disk of half gray and half black, separated diagonally. The left portion is gray, with the numeral "9" in black, and the right is black with the numeral "4" in white.

272. **Ninety-fifth Division**
A blue oval bearing the numeral "9" in red and the letter "V" in white intertwined in a monogram.

273. **Ninety-sixth Division**
Two overlapping diamond shapes, white at the left and blue at the right. The angles formed at the top and bottom are green. The patterns are on a khaki background.

274. **Ninety-seventh Division**
A blue shield with a wide white border; within it an upright vertical trident, in white.

246

247

248

249

250

251

252

253

254

255

256

257

258

AIRBORNE

259

260

261

262

263

264

265

275. Ninety-eighth Division
A blue shield, as used in New Amsterdam, with an orange border. Within this is the head of an Iroquois chief with five feathers, also in orange. The colors are those of the Dutch House of Nassau.

276. Ninety-ninth Division
A black shield, in the center of which is a horizontal band of white and blue squares, from the arms of William Pitt.

277. 100th Division
A medium blue shield, with the numerals "100" centered within. The top half of the numerals is white and the bottom half, gold.

278. 101st Airborne Division
A black eared shield. Within this is the head of a screaming eagle, in white, with a golden beak. The airborne tab above is black with gold letters.

279. 102nd Division
This consists of the letters "O" and "Z" in gold with gold arcs below, which represents the Ozark Mountains. All are on a blue disk.

280. 103rd Division
A disk bearing a giant cactus in green on a blue ground, with a yellow gold background.

281. 104th Division
A green disk, with the head of a timberwolf in silver.

282. 106th Division
A blue disk with narrow white and wide red outer borders; within it the head of a lion, front view, in yellow.

283. 108th Division
A red oval with a narrow yellow border; within it is a mace, also in yellow.

284. 119th Division
A black disk; within it are flames in red, with yellow edges. The black sometimes looks like navy blue.

285. 130th Division
A medium blue disk, within which is the figure of a flying serpent, in white, representing swift striking power.

266

267

268

269

270

271

272

273

274

275

276

277

278

279

280

281

282

283

284

285

286. **135th Airborne Division**
A yellow disk, within which is a black spider design. The airborne tab above is black, with yellow letters.

287. **141st Division**
A blue disk with a thistle, in white, on it.

288. **157th Division**
A blue disk; within it is a heraldic tiger in yellow, with red claws and tongue.

289. **Americal Division**
A shield of blue, with four five-pointed stars, in white, arranged in the form of the Southern Cross.

290. **First Cavalry Division**
A very large patch, a triangular Norman shield of yellow, bearing a horse's head and diagonal stripe, both black.

291. **Second Cavalry Division**
The same shape and extra large size as that of the First Cavalry Division. It is yellow with a chevron and two eight-pointed stars, both in blue.

292. **Third Cavalry Division**
A yellow shield with the numeral "3" in blue.

293. **Twenty-first Cavalry Division**
A yellow disk, centered within which is a stirrup in black. Within the stirrup is a prairie flower with a purple bud.

294. **Twenty-fourth Cavalry Division**
A yellow area shaped like a stirrup, within which is a stirrup in black. In the opening of this is a rosebud. The bud is red and the stem and leaves are green.

295. **Fifty-sixth Division**
A disk of khaki, within which is a gold five-pointed star. Superimposed on the star is a decorative cross design of red.

296. **Sixty-first Cavalry Division**
A triangular shield of yellow with a silhouetted horse's head framed by an inverted spur, both in black.

297. **Sixty-second Cavalry Division**
A shield of gray with an inner frame of blue. Within this is a six-armed cross of yellow and in the center of the cross is a blue cross botonée. The edge of the shield is gray.

298. Sixty-third Cavalry Division
A yellow square with a red cross saltier on it.

299. Sixty-fourth Cavalry Division
A black shield; within this is a yellow Indian flint arrowhead. On the arrowhead is a pioneer's coonskin cap and a cavalry saber, in black.

300. Sixty-fifth Cavalry Division
A yellow shield with a blue triangular center. Within this center is a cavalry lance in yellow, point up. The edge of the shield is in khaki.

301. Sixty-sixth Cavalry Division
A khaki disk; centered in this is a double six-pointed star with wide blue edges and a yellow center.

302. Antilles Department
Originally this was called the Puerto Rican Department. Its badge is a shield of yellow with a red border; within it is a silhouette of Morro Castle, in red.

303. Hawaiian Department
An octagon of red, with stylized "H," centered, in yellow.

304. Panama Canal Department
A shield of the old Spanish colors, red and yellow. The yellow center design is bordered by red. The badge is symbolic of the Isthmus of Panama.

305. Philippine Department
A blue oval, centered within which is a Sea Lion brandishing a sword. The design is all in white.

306. Army Ground Force
A horizontally striped red, white, and blue disk, with the stripes equally spaced and the blue uppermost.

307. Army Service Force
A white cloud formation within a red disk. Centered in the white is a five-pointed star of blue, one point up.

308. Replacement and School Command
A vertically striped red, yellow, and blue disk. The red is at the left, and the stripes are equally spaced.

309. General Headquarters Reserve
A white disk, within which is a smaller disk of equally

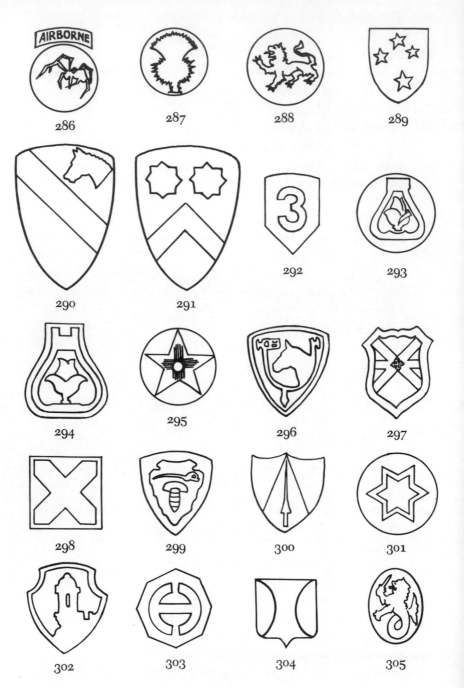

286

287

288

289

290

291

292

293

294

295

296

297

298

299

300

301

302

303

304

305

spaced, horizontal stripes of red, white, and blue, with the red at the top.

310. **Army Ground Forces Replacement Depots**

A dark blue center disk, with two circular border stripes, red at the edge and white within.

311. **First Army Group**

A light blue pentagon with narrow white and wide red borders. The red is at the edge. Within the light blue pentagon is the Roman numeral "I," in black.

312. **Sixth Army Group**

A red square, with six stripes of white interlaced.

313. **Headquarters, Twelfth Army Group**

An inverted stylized arrowhead with a wide black border. Within this border are horizontally divided areas of red, white, and blue, with the red at the top.

314. **Northwest Service Command**

A five-sided shape. The center stripe is white, with a five-pointed star of blue at the top. The stripes at either side are half red, half blue, with the blue at the top.

315. **Labrador, Northeast, and Central Canada Command**

A white disk. In the center is a horizontal red. Within this is an igloo of white with a blue doorway.

316. **Greenland Base Command**

A white disk, with a narrow red outer border. Within the disk are three wide wavy lines in blue which represent the sea.

317. **Southern Defense Command**

A large shield divided diagonally by a wide wavy line of white. The area at the top is red, and the bottom is blue.

318. **Eastern Defense Command**

A square shield, within which are crossed tridents and a wavy partition line. The line, tridents, and outer border are in yellow; the background of the top is red and of the bottom, blue.

319. **Caribbean Defense Command**

A blue disk bearing a galleon and waves in white. On the

306

307

308

309

310

311

312

313

314

315

316

317

318

319

320

321

322

323

324

325

sail is a red cross pattée; it resembles the sails used by Columbus when he explored this area.

320. **Atlantic Base Command**
A blue disk with a white inner border and a red outer border. Within the blue disk is a whale, in white.

321. **Headquarters, Southeast Asia Command**
A white disk with a narrow blue border, within which is a sea of flames, in red, at the bottom and a symbolic Phoenix, in blue, rising from the flames.

322. **Iceland Base Command**
A triangle representing an iceberg on an outer area of a disk, divided horizontally by a wavy line. The lower area is blue and the area of the iceberg (the triangle), white. The upper area of the disk is white, and the iceberg is red.

323. **Chinese Combat Training Command**
A white shield with three diagonally striped areas of red. Centered within this is a blue disk with the twelve-pointed star of China on it. This star has a lighter blue inner circle and twelve points.

324. **Bermuda Base Command**
A blue disk, centered within which is a white triangle with a red disk in the center. Three shell shapes in yellow are in the blue area.

325. **Airborne Command**
A red Norman shield, within which is a glider and an open parachute in white. The airborne tab is black with yellow lettering.

326. **Persian Gulf Service Command**
An Islamic green shield; within it a red sword is bordered in white, and above it is a white seven-pointed star, both from the flag of Iran.

327. **Antiaircraft Command**
A white disk with a very wide blue border. Within the white are the letters "AA" in red.

328. **Antiaircraft Artillery Command —
Western Defense Command**
A black diamond shape. The top area contains a yellow

sunset, and in the background there is a red sky area.

329. **Antiaircraft Artillery Command —**
Eastern Defense Command
A red three-sided shield and within this are the stylized letters "AAAC" in yellow, monogram-shaped.

330. **New England Frontier Defense Sector**
A khaki square, centered within which is a yellow disk. Superimposed on this is an artillery shell in red.

331. **New York–Philadelphia Frontier Defense Sector**
A khaki four-sided shape, with a smaller inner shape in yellow; superimposed upon this are two artillery shells in red.

332. **Chesapeake Bay Frontier Defense Sector**
A khaki disk, within which is centered a trefoil, in yellow. At the three joints of the trefoil are three artillery shells, in red.

333. **Antiaircraft Artillery Command —**
Central Defense Command
A shield like an Indian's in khaki. The top and bottom areas are composed of arrowheads in red, and superimposed on this are two crossed spears in yellow.

334. **Pacific Coastal Frontier Defense Sector**
A khaki disk bearing a nine-pointed star in yellow. Within this is an open inner circle. Centered on this, point up, is an artillery shell in red.

335. **Antiaircraft Artillery — Southern Defense Command**
A three-pointed flower design in khaki. The inner area shows three overlapping arrowheads in red. In each of them are three yellow arrows, points outward.

336. **Southern Coastal Frontier Defense Sector**
A khaki diamond with an inner diamond of yellow; superimposed upon it are four artillery shells in red.

337. **Military District of Washington, D.C.**
A blue oval with a narrow white border and a wider outer border of red. In the blue is the Washington Monument, in white on a green ground. Diagonally in front of the Monument is a double-handled sword in red, outlined in white, the handles in gold.

326

327

328

329

330

331

332

333

334

335

336

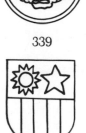

337

338

339

340

341

342

343

344

345

338. Armored Center and Units

A triangle containing equal areas of yellow, blue, and red. The yellow is at the top, and the blue is at the left. Centered at the juncture of the colors is a design of tank wheels and tracks and an artillery cannon, all in black, and a lightning bolt, in red. When the yellow area is blank it indicates Armored Center; if the area contains Roman numerals, they indicate the Armored Corps; and if the numerals are Gothic, they indicate the Armored Division.

339. Tank Destroyer Units

A yellow disk with a thin black border; centered in it is a black cougar crunching a tank in its jaws. The design is in black and red.

340. European Theater of Operations (Advance Base)

A blue oval, within which are lightning bolts in red with yellow borders, splitting chains of yellow. At the top is a white cloud area with a blue five-pointed star, which indicates advance base.

341. European Theater of Operations

The same as the above patch (340), without the star design above.

342. Supreme Headquarters, Allied Expeditionary Force

This is a black shield. The top contains a rainbow pattern. Below this is a broadsword in white, with a gold handle. The sword blade is flaming, and the flames are red.

343. China-Burma-India Theater

A shield with a blue chief; a twelve-pointed star of China in white at the left and a five-pointed star in white at the right. Below this arc five stripes of red and white, with the red at the edges.

344. Hawaiian Separate Coast Artillery Brigade

A red oval with a wide yellow border. Within this is an artillery shell in yellow with a hilly background in black behind it.

345. South Atlantic Force

Green and yellow wave patterns are at the base. Rising from the waves is a projection, in yellow, representing Ascension Island. A blue background is above, with five five-pointed white stars representing the Southern Cross. White, red, and light green form an outer frame on the sides and top.

346. Ports of Embarkation
A red shield; on it a helmsman's wheel in gold.

347. Middle East Zone
An inverted shield is framed in white. The lower portion contains waves of blue and white; the top part has a red sky and a five-pointed white star.

348. Hawaiian Coastal Defense
A yellow oval with a wide green border. Within this is a flower with green leaves and stem and red flower arms.

349. Panama Hellgate (Obsolete)
This patch was worn in the Panama Canal Zone prior to World War II. It is a red oval with a portcullis and chains in yellow and the word "Panama," above, also lettered in yellow.

350. North African Theater
A Moorish dome in white outlined in red. Within the dome is a five-pointed star in blue, one point up.

351. Army Amphibian Units
A blue patch with a curved top. The design on it consists of an anchor, an eagle, and a submachine gun in yellow.

352. Alaskan Defense Command
This disk depicts a snow scene, with a seal in black standing in front of an ice cap. Behind this is the midnight sun, radiating yellow to red, and in these rays are the letters "ADC" in black.

353. Alaskan Department
A blue disk showing the face of a white polar bear, its mouth in red. Above this is a five-pointed star in yellow, representing the North Star.

354. Allied Force Headquarters
A blue disk with a narrow red outline. The letters "AF" are in white in a center monogram.

346

347

348

349

350

351

352

353

354

355

356

357

358

359

360

361

362

363

364

365

355. Engineer Amphibian Command

A white oval, with a blue inner border. In the center is the figure of a sea horse in red.

356. Officer's Candidate School

A black disk with the letters "S" and "C" in a monogram within an "O," all in an olive drab color. This patch was worn on the lower sleeve.

357. Army Specialized Training Program

An eight-sided design in yellow with narrow blue edges. Within this are the lamp of knowledge and a sword, in blue. Where the sword joins the lamp it is yellow. The same patch within a yellow diamond indicates the Reserve.

358. Kiska Defense Force

A blue disk with a silver-gray border. Within this is a dagger (Bowie knife) of white with a black handle.

359. European Civil Affairs

A shield with five stripes, red in the center and white and blue at either side, with the blue at the edge. Within the center red stripe is a Roman sword of white with a gold handle, point up. The whole is framed in red.

360. Military Mission in Moscow

An inverted triangle with a rounded top. Within this is an American eagle in white, with a red, white, and blue shield on its chest. The background is red, with a white cloud line above the eagle, and then a blue area containing the Russian word for America in white, framed in white.

361. Task Force

A red shield with a narrow white border. Within the shield are the letter "V" and three dots and a dash, all in white.

The following three patches were worn on the front of the overseas cap.

362. Paratroops

A red or light blue disk with an open parachute in white and a wide border also in white. The blue is for infantry, and the red is for artillery.

363. **Glider Borne Troops**

A blue disk contains a glider plane, centered, in white. A wide border of light blue indicates infantry and red stands for artillery.

364. **Glider Borne Paratroops**

A blue disk with an open parachute and a glider plane, both in white, centered upon it. The border is light blue or red.

365. **Military Personnel — U.S. Military Academy**

A white shield with a red inner border. Centered in this, in blue, is the helmet of Pallas over a Greek sword. This is the emblem of West Point, the Military Academy.

366. **Ranger Battalion Tabs**

A black scroll with a thin red inner border. The word "Ranger" is in white in the center and to the left is the number of the battalion. To the right are the letters "BN," for battalion, also in white. The badge used by the First Battalion is shown, but there were six such battalion patches.

Another patch used by the Rangers was a black diamond shape with the word "Rangers" and a wide border in yellow. (Not shown.)

367. **Ninety-ninth Infantry Battalion**

A white shield with blue waves at the bottom; on them is a Viking ship, of blue, with nine shields of red and a sail of blue and red.

368. **442nd Regimental Combat Team**

The original patch. It is a red disk with a thin blue edge; in the center are a lei of yellow and a hand grasping a white sword.

369. **442nd Combat Team (New)**

This new patch is a six-sided shape of blue, with a narrow white inner frame and a wide red border. Within this is a hand holding the torch of Liberty, in white.

370. **First Special Service Force**

A red flint arrowhead inscribed "USA" and "Canada," in white.

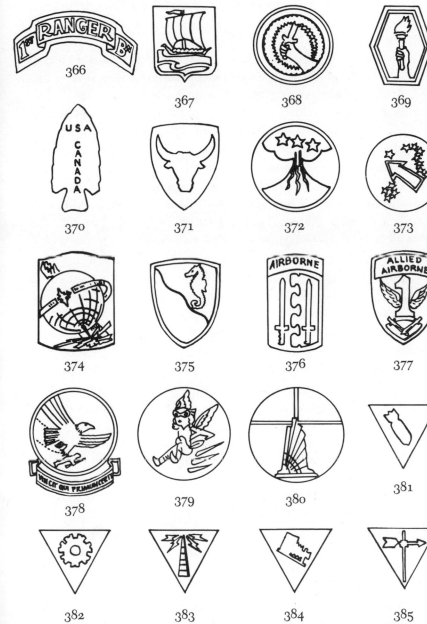

366

367

368

369

370

371

372

373

374

375

376

377

378

379

380

381

382

383

384

385

371. The Philippine Division

A red shield, with the head of a horned carabao, in yellow, centered.

372. First Filipino Unit

A yellow disk with a black volcanic mountain emitting black smoke, in which are three five-pointed yellow stars.

373. United States Army Forces Pacific Area

A blue disk, with a red arrow pointer, outlined in white. Surrounding this are twelve white five-pointed stars, as in the Southern Cross constellation.

374. Army Airways Communications Systems

A blue area, with a globe of the world in white. Encompassing this are a red band and an airplane in black. Behind this is a wing of gold, and at the bottom of the axis point of the globe are white lightning bolts.

375. Thirty-sixth Engineers

An unofficial patch. A shield half red, half white, connected by a wavy line. In the red is a sea horse in white. The shield is black-bordered.

376. Second Airborne Infantry Brigade

A squared shield, divided in half by interlocking joints. The right side is blue with a white sword, and the left side is white with a blue sword. The airborne tab above is black, with the letters in yellow.

377. First Allied Airborne

A gray-green shield. The top area is black with the words "Allied Airborne" in yellow. The large figure "1" is in white, with yellow wings. Below this is a red field with crossed Roman swords in white.

378. Air Troop Carriers

A black disk edged in gold with a flying eagle carrying a trooper, all in gold. A golden scroll is below, with the motto *"Vincit Qui Primum Gerit"* in black.

379. Women's Air Ferrying Command

A blue disk with the figure of a winged female gremlin wearing a flying helmet, in full color. Below are three clouds in white.

380. Air Carrier — Ground Personnel
A golden-tan disk, with a decorative wing on a base; above that are cross-hairs in deep red-brown.

The following patches are Army Air Forces Technical Specialists' insignia. They were worn low on the sleeve, near the cuff. They are all the same design, an inverted triangle of blue. The design centered within this is yellow, and it signifies the specialist's technical field.

381. Armament Specialist
The center design is an aerial bomb in yellow.

382. Engineering Specialist
The center design is an old-fashioned airplane engine without a propeller.

383. Communication Specialist
The center design is a communication tower, with four rays issuing from the top of the tower.

384. Photography Specialist
The center design is an aerial camera in yellow.

385. Weather Specialist
The center design is a weather vane with an arrow pointer.

The following patches are used by the United States Army Air Corps.

386. Army Air Force (Original)
An orange disk with a three-armed design symbolic of a spinning propeller, in dark blue.

387. Army Air Force
A dark blue disk. At the bottom is a five-pointed star in white, with a red disk center. At either side of the upper point of the star are golden wings.

388. Air Force Cadet
A black or dark blue disk. In the center is the insigne of the Air Corps, a pair of wings. Centered on this is a double-bladed airplane propeller.

389. First Air Force

A blue disk with a five-pointed star in white at the bottom. A red disk is in the center of the star and at either side are wings of gold. Between the outstretched wings is the numeral "1" in white.

390. Second Air Force

A blue square with a falcon in flight, in gold. Above is a five-pointed white star with a red disk in its center.

391. Third Air Force

A wide orange circle with a blue center. Within the center is the numeral "3" in white. Behind this is a ray of red. In the lower half of the numeral is the five-pointed white star with red disk center.

392. Fourth Air Force

A blue shield with a narrow orange border. At the top are wings in white with an open center containing a white star with red center. Below this are four rays of orange.

393. Fifth Air Force

A blue disk with the numeral "5" in orange. Behind this are a white comet with three tails and the constellation of the Southern Cross of five five-pointed stars, all in white. A star with a red center is within the ball of the comet.

394. Sixth Air Force

A blue hexagon, with a white five-pointed star with a red disk center at the bottom. Golden wings are at either side of the star. Above is a galleon in orange.

395. Seventh Air Force

A blue disk with an orange border. Within this is a white five-pointed star, projected, with red edges and center. Through the center is a large numeral "7" in orange.

396. Eighth Air Force

A blue disk, with an open figure "8" in orange. Wings appear at either side of the "8," in orange. Within the bottom of the "8" is a white star with a red center.

397. Ninth Air Force

A blue shield. In its lower section is an orange disk with the numeral "9" in red within it. Above and at either side are

386

387

388

389

390

391

392

393

394

395

396

397

398

399

400

401

402

403

404

large curved wings of white. Above and between the wings is a white star with a red disk center.

398. Tenth Air Force

A blue disk. At the bottom is a white shield with the numeral "10" in blue. On either side are large curved wings in orange. Above is a thin white circle, and within this is a white star with a red disk center.

399. Eleventh Air Force

A blue shield with a rounded bottom. At the left is a white five-pointed star with red center, and extending from this is a long, stylized wing of orange. At the upper left is the numeral "11" in red edged with white.

400. Twelfth Air Force

An inverted triangle of blue. Centered on it is a white five-pointed star with a red disk center. Near the top of the star at either side are wings of orange, flared out to the edges.

401. Thirteenth Air Force

A blue disk with a narrow orange edge. At the top is the numeral "13" in white. Below this is a white five-pointed star with red center, and at either side are decorative wings of orange and red.

402. Fourteenth Air Force

A blue disk. This patch was adopted from the famous Flying Tigers, and it depicts a flying tiger with wings in orange and black. Above this is a white five-pointed star with a red disk center.

403. Fifteenth Air Force

A blue disk with a narrow inner circle of orange. At the top is the numeral "15" in orange. At the bottom is a white star with a red disk center, and at either side of the star are wings of orange.

404. Twentieth Air Force

A blue disk with white crosslines, signifying the globe. Near the top is a white numeral "20." At the bottom is an orange circle, with wings of orange at either side. Within the circle is a white five-pointed star with a red disk center.

405. Air Transport Command
A large silver disk with a polar view of the world in the lower part. In front of this is a wing-shaped device in black and red, and at the left edge are colored sections like ribbon bars.
Ferry Command
The same insigne, except that the disk is gold. (Not shown.)

406. U.S.A.A.F. Instructor
A blue disk with a narrow yellow border. Within this is a white five-pointed star with a red disk center. Between the arms of the star are the letters "USAFI" in yellow.

407. Mediterranean Allied Air Forces
A blue rectangle with rounded edges and a thin narrow inner border of orange. At the top is a pair of wings in white. Below this are the letters "MAAF" in orange. Behind the letters is a series of wavy lines in white.

408. U.S.A.F. Headquarters Command
A dark blue disk, with a wide inner border of alternating lines of pale yellow and light blue. Centered within this is the Capitol dome in white.

409. Air University
A blue disk. At the top, in orange, is the lamp of knowledge. Below this are the letters "UA" in white in monogram form. Within the letters is a white five-pointed star with red disk center, and at either side of the letters are wide wings in orange.

410. Air Reserve Officers' Training Corps
A blue shape, with the white, five-pointed Air Force star with a red center in the lower portion. Orange wings are above and at either side of the star. The inscription "Air R.O.T.C." is in orange at the top.

411. Ninth Air Engineer Command
A blue shield with the Roman numeral "IX" in orange at the top. Below this is a five-pointed star of white with red center and wings of orange at either side. Above the center and superimposed on the wings is a red disk with white crossed lines symbolic of airfields.

412. Air Matériel Command

A blue disk. At the bottom is a cogwheel in white. Centered in this is a white five-pointed star with a red disk center. At either side are widely spread wings of orange.

413. Airborne Troop Carrier

A blue shield, with the white five-pointed star and red disk center, and the wide-spread wings of orange of the Air Force. Within the wings are an open parachute and glider in white. Above these are the words "Troop Carrier" in orange. The airborne tab is black, with yellow letters.

414. Air Technical Service Command in Europe

A blue disk with an orange cogwheel. Within the cog are the letters, "ATSCE" in white and below this is the white five-pointed star with red center. At either side are the spread wings of orange.

415. Air Forces in Europe

A blue disk with a white five-pointed star with a red disk center at the bottom. Widely spread wings of orange are at either side. Centered above the star is a flaming broadsword with a gold handle and white blade. The flames are in red.

416. Alaska Air Command

This is a blue shield. At the top left is a five-pointed star of white with red center and extending from this is a long single wing of orange. Below this are five-pointed stars in the Big Dipper formation, also in orange.

417. Military Air Transport — Eastern Air Defense

A blue disk; centered in it is a pair of golden wings. In the center are three crossed arrows. Behind this are cross sections of white resembling a globe of the world.

418. Air Training Command

A blue disk; within this is an elongated five-pointed star of white. A torch is centered on a set of wings in orange and passes through the star. The base is yellow and the flame is red.

419. Far East Air Force — Pacific Air Command

This is a blue diamond shape and centered in this is a white

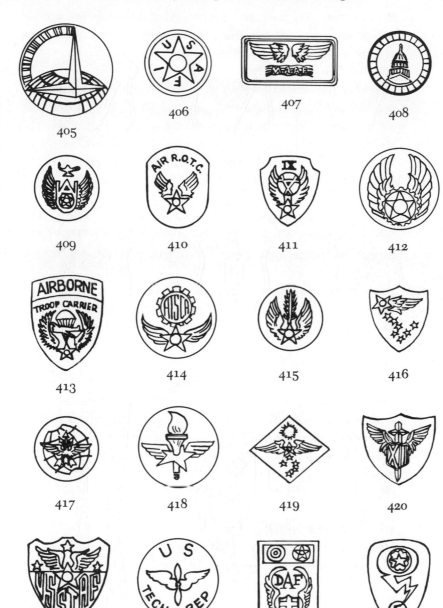

405

406

407

408

409

410

411

412

413

414

415

416

417

418

419

420

421

422

423

424

five-pointed star with red center. At either side are spread wings of orange. Above this is a sunburst in gold and below are five five-pointed stars in white.

420. Twelfth Tactical Air Force

A wide blue shield; within it is the outline of a shield in orange. In this is the Roman numeral "XII" in white and at either side of the shield are spread wings of orange. The whole design is superimposed upon a vertical stylized sword of yellow and orange. The shield is sometimes black.

421. United States Strategic Air Force

A large shield. The chief, or upper part, is in blue, with three white five-pointed stars and orange-colored wings. The lower section is white, with the stylized letters "USSTAF" in red. Atop the letters is a white five-pointed star with a red center.

422. United States Technical Representative

A blue disk with a silver, double-bladed propeller, flanked at either side by gold wings. The inscription "US Tech Rep" is in gold.

423. Desert Air Force

A large shield of dark blue. At the top is a light gray rectangle with air markings for the Allies, Britain and the United States. At the left is a cockade with a red center, white, and then blue at the edge. At the right is a blue disk with a white five-pointed star with a red center. At the bottom of the dark blue shield is a Norman-type shield of gray, with a golden cross in the center. Long decorative wings of orange are at either side of this shield. Within the wings are the letters "DAF" in red.

424. Manhattan Project — Atomic Bomb

This was never an official patch. It is a blue shape with rounded ends. At the top is a large cloud with a lightning bolt descending from it. Both are in white. In the cloud is the insigne of the Army Service Force in red, white, and blue. The tip of the lightning bolt is splitting a yellow globe.

425. Fourteenth Antiaircraft Command

A white disk, with a wide blue outer border. Within the

blue border are fourteen five-pointed stars in white. Within the white center disk are the letters "AA" in red as a monogram.

426. **Army Reserve Officers' Training Corps**

A horizontally striped red, white, and blue disk, with the red at the bottom. Superimposed upon this is a flaming torch in yellow. In the red at the bottom is the inscription "Army R.O.T.C." in yellow.

427. **Guam Detachment — Marianas Bonin Command**

This badge is a large decorative shield with a narrow red border. Within it is a tropical scene of a palm tree, lagoon, sailing native bark, and sandy beach, all in color. The word "Guam," centered, is in red.

428. **Guam (New)**

A disk with a narrow red border; within it is a palm tree in full color with a white sky and blue sea behind it.

429. **Forty-sixth Division**

A blue Norman shield showing a mailed fist in yellow.

430. **Forty-seventh Division**

A blue disk, with thin white and wide red outer borders. The red is at the edge. Within the blue is a Viking helmet in white.

431. **Forty-eighth Division**

A four-pointed star, separated into eight sections of red and white (four of each color). The star is edged in black.

432. **Forty-ninth Division**

A shield, separated diagonally into red and yellow, with the yellow at the top. Superimposed on this is the figure of a Forty-niner or gold miner, panning for gold, in blue.

433. **Fifty-first Division**

A pentagon shape, divided in half, vertically, with blue at the left and yellow at the right. Upon this is a rattlesnake in black and white.

434. **108th Airborne Division**

A seven-sided shape in red. Within this is the figure of a winged griffin in yellow. The airborne patch is black with yellow letters.

425

426

427

428

429

430

431

432

433

434

435

436

437

438

439

440

441

442

443

444

435. Fourth Cavalry Group
A wide yellow shield with a blue center section. Within this is a field cannon, point down, in yellow. Crossed in front of this are a cavalry saber and early-style bayonet in red. Behind the blue center stripe is a cavalry saber in red.

436. Sixth Cavalry Group
A decorative shield in dark blue, with a thin yellow inner border. Within this is a stylized rearing horse in yellow.

437. Western Pacific — Far East Command
A red disk with a centered white cloud formation. A lightning bolt of yellow crosses diagonally. In back of this is a large five-pointed star in the center, and about it are five smaller five-pointed stars, all in blue.

438. General Headquarters — South West Pacific
An olive drab square with a blue flag. The flag is edged in yellow with a yellow staff. Within the flag are the letters "GHQ" in a yellow monogram.

439. Ryukyus Command
A black disk with a narrow gold border. Within this is an Oriental archway, also in gold.

440. European Headquarters — ETO
A large blue shield edged in gold. In the chief are bands of blue, white, and red with the red at the bottom. Below this is a gold stylized eagle, with wings spread, surrounded by thirteen five-pointed stars of white.

441. Merrill's Marauders (5307 Composite Unit)
This is a large shield, all on a blue ground. It has a narrow red border and is separated into quarters of green and blue. In the blue, top left, is the Chinese star in white. In the blue, bottom right, is the American star in white. Diagonally across the shield is a lightning bolt in red. The patch at the top is blue, edged in red, with the words "Merrill's Marauders" in two lines, in red.

442. Trieste Forces
A cloverleaf design in blue, with white edges. Within this is a red shield with a white fleur-de-lis. The tab above is blue, edged in white, with the word "Trust" in white.

443. Korea Military Advisory Group

This is a Korean bell in blue with a white and red decoration at the top, and a red strip edged in white below. A flying eagle in white is centered in this. A blue tab with white letters "KMAG" (not shown) was worn below this.

444. Berlin District

A yellow shield edged in black. Within this is the Brandenburg Gate in black, symbolizing Berlin.

MARINE CORPS SHOULDER INSIGNIA, 1918-1947

THE FOLLOWING PATCHES were worn by members of the United States Marine Corps from 1918 to 1947. The use of distinctive shoulder insignia was abolished by the Marine Corps in a Letter of Instruction, September 23, 1947.

445. Marine Brigade — Second Army Division, A.E.F.

The patch shown was used by the Fifth Marine Regiment. The Sixth Marine Regiment used the same design in a diamond shape. The design is a white five-pointed star, one point up, with the head of an Indian in full war bonnet centered within. The color of the background on which the star was placed shows the battalion: black, Headquarters; green, Supply; purple, Machine Gun Company; red, First Battalion; yellow, Second Battalion; and blue, Third Battalion.

446. Fifth Marine Brigade — A.E.F.

This was an unofficial patch. It was a black disk, with the Marine Corps emblem of a globe, anchor, and eagle in red, with the Roman numeral "V" in black in the center of the globe.

447. Marine Detachment — Iceland

This patch was unofficial. The British authorities, as a gesture, presented several thousand polar bear patches to the Marines when they landed in Iceland. This is a black rectangle with a rounded top. Within this is a polar bear in white (some were in silver).

448. First Marine Division

A diamond shape of medium blue; centered in it is a red numeral "1," edged in white. The name "Guadalcanal" is in white within the blue field. Five five-pointed stars in white are in the shape of the Southern Cross constellation.

449. Second Marine Division

An arrow head of scarlet, with a white hand holding a golden torch. On the torch is a "2" in scarlet. In the scarlet field are five white stars, as in the Southern Cross.

450. Third Marine Division

This is a scarlet shield with a thin gold inner frame. Centered in the scarlet is a three-armed device, separated into alternating black and gold.

451. Fourth Marine Division

This is a scarlet diamond shape with the numeral "4" in gold, edged in thin white.

452. Fifth Marine Division

Shown is a scarlet shield with a gold inner frame. Centered in the scarlet is the Roman numeral "V" in gold. Superimposed on this is a spearhead of black.

453. Sixth Marine Division

This features a blue disk with a white sword, point up, in the center. Superimposed on this is the numeral "6" in gold, edged in scarlet. Around the blue is a wide red band, with the words, "Melanesia * Micronesia * Orient *," separated by stars done in gold.

454. First Marine Amphibious Corps

This shield is in blue with a red diamond center edged in white. Five white stars in the Southern Cross constellation surround the center. The diamond in the center has different insignia in white upon it for the different battalions within the Corps: Open parachute, Paratroopers; a winged castle, Flight Engineers; white star, Supply; human skull, Raiders; barrage balloon, Barrage Balloon Sections; anti-aircraft gun, Defense Battalions.

455. Third Amphibious Corps

This is a wide shield of scarlet, with the mystic sea monster

445

446

447

448

449

450

451

452

453

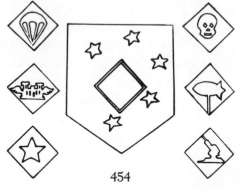

454

455

of the Scriptures in gold, outlined in black. Above this near the top is the Roman numeral "III" in white.

456. Fifth Amphibious Corps

A scarlet shield, with the head of an alligator in gold and black. Above this are three five-pointed white stars in a line.

457. Fleet Marine Force — Pacific

This is a scarlet shield with the top composed of the upper half of an eagle with wings spread. The head is in white and its outline and the shield are edged in gold. The letters "FMF — PAC" are in white, separated by narrow white lines. In the center of the shield is a gold disk and within this is a mailed fist grasping lightning bolts, all in scarlet. Three five-pointed stars in white complete the design. This patch is for the Headquarters Detachment. The center device is different for each separate unit: dog's head is for Dog Platoons; field cannon, Artillery Battalions; white star, Supply; armored tractor, Amphibious Tractor Battalions; castle, Separate Engineer Battalions; an aerial bomb, Bomb Disposal Companies; antiaircraft gun, Antiaircraft Artillery; an amphibian personnel carrier, DUKW ("Duck") Companies.

458. Ship's Detachments

A scarlet diamond, with a blue anchor and a golden sea horse superimposed on it.

459. Headquarters, Marine Air Wing — Pacific

A scarlet shield. At the top are two gold stars, in the center is a pair of gold wings, and below is a golden coronet (crown). The following patch (460) was adopted, and this patch became obsolete.

460. Headquarters, Pacific Air Wing

An elongated diamond in scarlet, with the Marine Corps insigne in gold and black. Wings are at either side in gold and the letters "PAC" are at the bottom in black. Roman numerals in black replaced the letters for the air wings.

461. Eighteenth Defense Battalion

A scarlet crusader's shield, with a wide broadsword, point

456

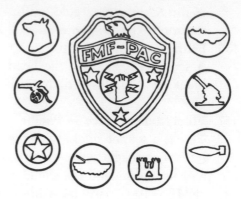

457

458

459

460

461

462

463

464

465

466

up, in white. Behind this are gold wings. At either side of the sword are the numerals "1" and "8" in extended black figures.

462. Fifty-first Defense Battalion

A red disk, with large numerals "51" in white. Superimposed on these is an antiaircraft gun in dark blue. Below are the letters "USMC" in white.

463. Fifty-second Defense Battalion

Shown is a scarlet shield with a wide white border, separated diagonally by a blue stripe, with four white stars within it. Behind this is a field gun, firing, in gold. At the base of the gun are the letters "USMC" in scarlet, and above, within a shellburst of gold, is the numeral "52" in scarlet.

The following three patches were never officially adopted.

464. Second Marine Division

A blue diamond, edged in white, with a snake in the form of the letter "S" in scarlet. The word "Guadalcanal" is in gold within the snake. Five white stars, as in the Southern Cross, complete the design.

465. Thirteenth Defense Battalion

A shield, divided diagonally in red, white, and blue. Within this is centered a sea horse of green, and the letters "FMF" in white appear on it.

466. Marine Detachment — Londonderry, Northern Ireland

A scarlet shield, with a small inner frame of gold. Centered at the top is a Marine Corps emblem in gold and black, and below this is a shamrock of green.

The following patches were adopted and used by the naval services during World War II. None of these is in use today.

467. Construction Battalions (Seabees)

This is the original patch adopted by the Naval Construction battalions. It is a blue disk with a wide white border. Within the blue, a bee with a sailor hat on is carrying tools and a submachine gun. Below this are the letters "CB" in white.

468. Construction Battalions (New)

This is the same as the original patch (467), but the bee is slightly larger, and the word "Seabees" in white appears below the bee.

469. Patrol Torpedo Boats (First Type)

A dark blue disk with a thin inner border of white. Within this is a mosquito riding a torpedo over waves, all in white. This refers to the name originally given to the PT boats, mosquito boats.

470. Patrol Torpedo Boats (Second Type)

A navy blue disk with a white rope border. Diagonally across this is a torpedo and its wake, and above and to the left are the letters "PT," all in white.

471. Harbor Net Tender

A navy blue disk, with a white rope border. Within this is an octopus with a sailor hat on its head. It is grabbing a submarine in its tentacles. The whole design is white on the blue.

472. Naval Amphibious Forces

A large patch with round top of scarlet. Within this is a design that consists of an anchor, an eagle with wings spread, and a submachine gun, all carried out in gold.

473. Naval Amphibious Forces (Original)

This was the first design used, a disk showing a wide blue border, green water, and tan shoreline, and an alligator in full colors. Tanks are coming from its open jaws onto the beach.

474. Minecraft Personnel

A disk with a dark blue border. The bottom half is light blue and the sky area yellow. A floating mine is in black and its explosive points are in yellow. From the mine radiate lightning bolts of red.

475. Navy V-5 Training Program

A shield of yellow. The chief has a navy blue rectangular shape, with the word "Navy" in yellow. At the bottom is

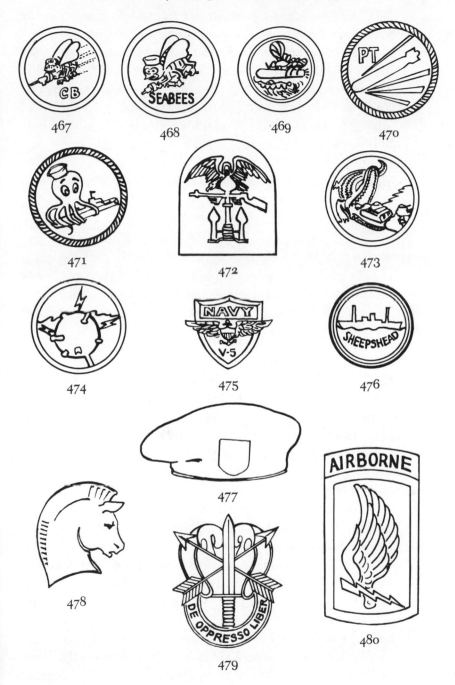

467

468

469

470

471

472

473

474

475

476

477

478

479

480

"V-5" in blue. Superimposed on this shield are a pair of naval flyer's wings in yellow, outlined in navy blue.

476. **U.S. Maritime School (U.S. Merchant Marine)**
A disk with a thin red, blue, and white border. Centered in this is a freighter-type ship in white. The upper background is red and the sea area below is dark blue with the word "Sheepshead" in white. (The school was at Sheepshead Bay, New York.)

With the beginning of the Cold War at the close of World War II, and, more important, after the end of the Korean War, the Army decided that some sort of special units, small, well trained, and hard hitting, should operate behind enemy lines, much like some of the Rangers or Raiders of World War II.

In 1952 just such special units were formed, and the name adopted was the Special Forces. Some means was sought to give the elite Special Forces a distinctive type of insigne, and the green beret was adopted.

477. **Special Forces Green Beret**
This is the first time that an article of clothing has been used in place of a shoulder insigne to show a man's unit. Centered in the green beret is a shield-shaped patch known as a "flash," which is a different color for each Special Forces group and designates the wearer's group. The red flash most often seen is for the Seventh Special Forces Group serving in Vietnam.
The flash was originally worn on the left side, above the ear, but is now worn directly over the left eye.

478. **Special Forces Crest (Obsolete)**
This was the original crest of the Special Forces and was worn centered on the flash. It is the head of a Trojan Horse, signifying the nature of surprise used by the Special Forces. It is in silver.

479. **Special Forces Crest**
This badge is now worn by the Special Forces on the beret flash. It is made of crossed arrows in silver (the original

crest of the First Special Forces units, United States Army, during World War II). Centered upon this is an Army field knife, in silver, with a black handle, point up. Behind this is a ribbon device in black, edged in silver, scrolled at the top in silver, and below is the motto of the Special Forces, *"De Oppresso Liber"* ("To Liberate from Oppression"), worked in silver. This badge is now worn upon the beret flash, above the left eye.

480. First Airborne Infantry Division

This patch was originally worn by members of the 173rd Airborne Brigade (Separate) and then adopted by this unit when it was enlarged to make up a new division of the Army. The insigne is a patch of blue with straight sides and rounded top and bottom; completely enclosing this is a wide band of white and centered within this is a large wing in white, with a lightning bolt of red diagonally across the bottom. Atop the patch is the Airborne patch in blue with the word "Airborne" in white.

PART V

Army
Distinctive Insignia

1

2

3

4

5

6

7

8

9

10

11

12

13

14

15

16

17

18

19

20

THESE DISTINCTIVE INSIGNIA are often incorrectly called regimental insignia, perhaps because these crests were originally used only in that way. During and after World War II, however, thousands of designs were authorized and adopted for units as small as companies and battalions.

Because there have been many thousands of distinctive insignia in use from the past to the present day, it would be impossible to include them all in a work of this nature. However, the insignia of most of the infantry line regiments of the regular and reserve establishments of the Army and of the National Guard are included, and the wide variety of such insignia is indicated by some of the more unusual services which employ such badges.

The designs are enameled on metal. Usually officers wear them on shoulder loops and enlisted men wear them on service coat lapels. Prior to World War II, however, these badges were worn on campaign hats and garrison caps, and I have seen them worn on field scarves. Evidently the wearing of such insignia was and is left to the discretion of unit and field commanders.

Distinctive insignia follow the laws of heraldry more closely than any other type of insignia for the United States armed forces. Some specific rules apply. For instance, no part of the coat of arms of the United States, or any complete arms, seal, or flag of any state or country may be used. A metal design may not be placed on metal or a color used on a color. All symbols, whether animals, birds, or inanimate figures, must face the honorable — that is, the dexter, or right — side.

Many of the symbols in use show what campaign or war the unit served in. For example, a red cross of St. George indicates service in the Revolutionary War, and a pine tree symbolizes service by troops from New England in the same war. A maple leaf is for service in the War of 1812. Civil War service is shown by a blue saltier from the Confederate flag. This same design with white stars in it usually symbolizes service by the Confederate forces in the same war. Crossed arrows or arrows and a quiver, or an Indian tepee signify service in the Indian wars. Mexican War service and service at the Mexican border are usually indicated by a cactus. Service in the Spanish-American War is indicated by the Spanish colors, yellow and red; a five-bastioned fort; a battlement of Morro Castle; or San Juan Hill outpost. Philippine Insurrection service is indicated by a native bolo knife or machete; service in the Hawaiian Islands by a taro leaf; and service in the Boxer Rebellion in China (1900) by a Chinese dragon. World War I service is indicated, as is service in France, by a fleur-de-lis, and/or a battle honor. Many times, the work of the organization is represented, as by a parachute for airborne outfits or by a coastline for coast artillery.

The colors used are usually indicative of the type of organization, such as blue for infantry, red for artillery, and yellow for cavalry.

1. **First Infantry Regiment**
   A decorative shield with a diagonal band of fourteen notches across the shield. The upper part is red and the lower part, blue. The band is silver on gold, edged in black. Around this, in a circular design of gold and black, is a border and within this is the regiment's motto, "*Semper Primus*" ("Always First"), in black.

2. **Second Infantry Regiment**
   A gold shield, with a blue saltier (like a St. Andrew's cross), centered. Within this are crossed arrows and quiver and a bolo knife. At the left is a red cross pattée, below is a cactus, and to the right is a five-bastioned fort. Below it in a scroll, is the motto "*Noli Me Tangere*" ("Touch Me Not").
   Third Infantry Regiment
   No badge is worn by this unit. Instead, a black leather strap

with buff leather woven into it is worn on the left shoulder. (Not shown.)

Fourth Infantry Regiment

No badge is worn by this unit. Instead, a strip of scarlet cloth with a green stripe in the center is worn as a band in the coat shoulder loop. (Not shown.)

3. **Fifth Infantry Regiment**

   This is a large gold shield with the regimental coat of arms; the inner shield is bordered in red, green, and white. The center is separated by a wide red band with an Indian arrow on it. Above are four field cannons; below, three cannons. Above this is an arm in armor grasping nine arrows, and below it is a scroll with the motto "I'll Try, Sir."

4. **Sixth Infantry Regiment**

   A decorative shield, white at the bottom, with a scaling ladder in green. Above this is an alligator in green. The top part of the shield has a silver cross on a red field, and below this on a scroll is the motto "Unity Is Strength."

5. **Seventh Infantry Regiment**

   This circular scroll is blue edged in gold with the motto in gold letters, *"Volens et Potens"* ("Willing and Able"). Centered upon this are crossed bayonets of the Revolutionary War period behind a cotton bale.

6. **Eighth Infantry Regiment**

   This decorative shield is mounted and framed in high relief in gold. The shield is white and has a blue diagonal band with three flowers on it. At the right are a crossed arrow and tomahawk, and at the left is the claw of an eagle. The shield is shaped like a Spanish coat of arms, and the whole is surmounted by a crown.

7. **Ninth Infantry Regiment**

   A circular disk, with the numeral "9" centered, and below it the motto of the regiment, "Keep Up the Fire." The whole is surrounded and completely encircled by a five-toed Imperial Chinese dragon. The badge is in gold.

8. **Tenth Infantry Regiment**

   A Roman numeral "X" in blue superimposed on a sheathed

Roman sword in gold. In front of this is a silver circular band with the motto "Courage and Fidelity" and "MDCCLV" in blue.

9. **Eleventh Infantry Regiment**
The upper half of this shield is in silver, with a red cross, and the lower section is in blue bordered by a battlement. Within the lower section are a castle and an arrow above a crossed bolo knife and Philippine *campilan* knife, all in silver and gold.

10. **Twelfth Infantry Regiment**
A shield with a gold upper half and a blue lower half. In the upper section are a sea lion and a sword in red. In the blue lower section an Indian wigwam, in full color, is centered. Above and at either side are silver moline crosses edged in gold.

11. **Thirteenth Infantry Regiment**
A shield of blue and white stripes with a red cross saltier in the center; at either side are Civil War general's shoulder straps. At the top are two palm branches, and in front of them is a cartridge box with the words "Forty Rounds," which resembles the corps badge for the Fifteenth Army Corps during the Civil War. Below this is a scroll with the motto "First at Vicksburg."

12. **Fourteenth Infantry Regiment**
A gold Imperial Chinese dragon placed against a red conventionalized Spanish castle. Behind and below this is a blue ribbon scroll, with the motto "The Right of the Line" in gold letters.

13. **Fifteenth Infantry Regiment**
A decorative shield, white at the top and blue at the bottom. In the white portion at the top, are four acorns, taken from the Fourteenth Army Corps Badge of the Civil War, and a rock formation, representing the Rock of Chickamauga, from that same war. This is within a triangular shape. Below, in the blue section, is a Chinese Imperial dragon in gold. At the bottom of the shield is a scroll in gold with the motto "Can Do" in black.

14. Sixteenth Infantry Regiment

A shield of white and blue, known as a fur vair, based on the arms of Fleville, France, where the regiment fought in World War I. It consists of shields and inverted shields of white and blue, seventeen of each. Superimposed on the shield are an Indian arrow and Philippine bolo knife in gold, crossed. Below them is a five-bastioned fort in red.

15. Eighteenth Infantry Regiment

A shield; the upper section is white with a diagonal stripe of red. At either side are fleurs-de-lis in blue; the lower section is in blue with a white saltier in the center; at the top are crossed Indian arrows; at the left is a figure "8," and at the right is a bolo knife. Below this is a scroll with the motto "In Omnia Paratus" ("In All Things Prepared").

16. Nineteenth Infantry Regiment

A decorative blue shield edged in gold. Within this an infantry bugle of the Civil War period in gold; in the bend is the numeral "19" in white. Above this are three white five-pointed stars. Below the shield is a gold scroll with the motto "The Rock of Chickamauga" in blue.

17. Twentieth Infantry Regiment

A wreath or bar of three gold and three blue sections. Above the wreath are muskets in gold, crossed in pairs, forming the Roman numeral "XX."

18. Twenty-first Infantry Regiment

A shield, half white and half blue. In the blue at the top, a sunburst in gold, with a five-bastioned fort in blue centered on it. In the white below is a cedar tree in green. Above this is a blue and white wreath, and above this in turn, four arrows knotted by a rattlesnake. Below this is a blue scroll, edged in gold, with the motto "Duty" in gold.

19. Twenty-second Infantry Regiment

A shield, half blue and half white. In the white section at the top are five crossed Indian arrows knotted at the center. The blue section below is edged as with battlements, and centered upon it is a sunburst in gold, with the face of the sun in black.

20. **Twenty-third Infantry Regiment**

   A shield, blue at the top, with a white mountain peak at the bottom representing Mont Blanc during World War I. In the blue to the left is a white Maltese cross from the Fifth Corps Badge of the Civil War. To the right is a sea lion in gold and white from the seal of Manila. In the white area below is a globe of the world with the figures of a totem pole. There is a bear at the left and an eagle at the right, taken from the regiment coat of arms.

21. **Twenty-fourth Infantry Regiment**

   A blue disk completely encircled by yellow with a yellow scroll at the bottom. Within the disk is a blockhouse with a tower. The walls and masonry are in gray, and the roofs in yellow. Above this is a yellow scroll, with the words "San Juan" in blue. In the scroll at the bottom is the motto *"Semper Paratus"* ("Always Prepared") in blue.

22. **Twenty-fifth Armored Infantry Battalion (Old Twenty-fifth Infantry)**

   This is a blue shield edged in gold. Centered within this is the blockhouse of El Caney, Cuba, recalling the Spanish-American War. Behind this is a royal palm tree in green with a yellow trunk. Below, on a gold scroll, is the motto "Onward" in blue letters.

23. **Twenty-sixth Infantry Regiment**

   This white shield, edged in gold, has a Mohawk Indian arrowhead in blue, point up, also edged in gold.

24. **Twenty-seventh Infantry Regiment**

   A black oblong with rounded edges, bordered in gold. Within it is a wolf's head in gold, and below it is the motto *"Nec Aspera Terrent"* ("Frightened by No Difficulties"), also in gold.

25. **Twenty-eighth Infantry Regiment**

   A white shield, with a black rampant lion. It is derived from the arms of Picardy, France, where the regiment fought in World War I.

26. **Twenty-ninth Infantry Regiment**

   A shield with a white top, bordered in gold, and a mango

21

22

23

24

25

26

27

28

29

30

31

32

33

34

35

36

37

38

39

40

41

tree in green. The area below is blue with a bolo knife and a bayonet, crossed, in gold and silver. Above the shield is a wreath of blue and white, and atop this is the classic lamp of knowledge in gold. There is a white scroll below with the motto "We Lead the Way" in black.

27. **Thirtieth Infantry Regiment**

A wide circular disk in silver, with the motto "Our Country, Not Ourselves" at the top, and "Rock of the Marne, July 14-18, 1918" in black at the bottom. Within this circular band is a shield of silver and in the upper lefthand corner is the shoulder insigne of the Third Division, four blue diagonal stripes. Below this is a broken chevron in blue, and atop the shield is a wreath in blue and white. Above the shield is a boar's head in black.

28. **Thirty-first Infantry Regiment**

A polar bear facing right, in white and black, around which is a wreath of blue and white. Below this is a blue scroll edged in silver, with the motto *"Pro Patria"* ("For Country") in silver.

29. **Thirty-second Infantry Regiment**

This is a blue shield, in the upper lefthand corner of which is a white area with a red lion. Centered in the shield is a white saltier cross, and superimposed on this is a *puela* from the Hawaiian royal arms, all in gold. Above this is a wreath of blue and white, and atop this is an ancient Hawaiian war bonnet known as a *mahiole* in gold and red.

30. **Thirty-third Infantry Regiment**

A silver shield, with an inverted chevron of blue, is edged in white and blue. Within the area at the topmost section is a military bayonet in silver, and below is a decorative scroll with the motto *"Ridentes Venimus"* ("Smiling We Come").

31. **Thirty-sixth Armored Infantry Battalion
(Old Thirty-sixth Infantry)**

Above a wreath of blue and gold is a six-bastioned fort in green edged in gold, with a white five-pointed star centered within it.

32. **Thirty-seventh Infantry Regiment**

A blue shield with a center wavy white stripe and, in the top half of the blue section, a white five-pointed star. Below the shield is a scroll in white with the motto "For Freedom" in blue.

33. **Thirty-eighth Infantry Regiment**

This very decorative blue shield is edged in gold, with a gold scroll at the bottom. Within the shield is an inverted broken chevron of white, and below this are three bands of white, running diagonally. Above the shield is a wreath of blue and white and atop this is a rock formation. In the gold scroll at the bottom appears the motto "The Rock of the Marne" in blue.

34. **Forty-first Armored Infantry Battalion**
   (Old Forty-first Infantry)

A blue shield with a wide gold circular band and blue at the center. Within this is a fortress tower in silver and black. In the upper lefthand corner of the shield is a white square, and within this is a six-bastioned fort of green with a white five-pointed star. Below the shield is a scroll in silver with the motto "Straight and Stalwart" in black.

35. **Forty-seventh Infantry Regiment**

This white shield, edged in gold, has a square of blue with an Imperial Chinese five-toed dragon in gold in the upper lefthand corner. In the white area, and centered, is the shoulder sleeve insigne of the Fourth Division (A four-leafed design of ivy leaves in green).

36. **Fifty-first Infantry Regiment**

A blue shield with a gold band from the coat of arms of Alsace; below it, a blue scroll with "I serve" in white.

37. **Fifty-third Infantry Regiment**

This features an upright mace in gold with a blue scroll twined around the handle bearing the motto *"Courage sans Peur"* ("Courage without Fear") in gold.

38. **Fifty-fourth Armored Infantry Battalion**
   (Old Fifty-fourth Infantry)

This blue shield is edged in gold, and has a bend in gold

crossing it diagonally. To the left is a ragged tree trunk, and to the right in the corner is a white square with a scaling ladder in green.

39. **Sixtieth Infantry Regiment**

This black shield has a white, wide vertical line in the center, and centered in this is a red diamond, the Fifth Division insigne. In the lefthand corner is an embattlement in white with a field gun in green. Below this shield is a scroll in silver with the motto "To the Utmost Extent of Our Power" in black.

40. **Sixty-fifth Infantry Regiment**

This is a black Norman shield edged in gold with a Maltese cross in white, which is also edged in gold and centered thereon.

41. **Seventy-first Infantry Regiment**

This very decorative blue shield is edged in gold, and has, centered, a fasces between two upturned crescents. It is all in gold or yellow.

42. **Eighty-fifth Infantry Regiment**

This shield has a blue upper section with a ram's head in white and silver. The white section at the bottom is shaped like three mountain peaks; in this area is a jackboot with spur in green. Below the shield is a scroll in blue with the motto "Fix Bayonets" in white.

43. **104th Infantry Regiment (Massachusetts National Guard)**

This blue shield has an inverted chevron of white with a red cross within it. In the blue area is a torch and at either side are three five-pointed stars in white. At the bottom corner, below the torch, is an Indian arrowhead, all in white.

44. **105th Infantry Regiment (New York National Guard)**

This shield has the top half in blue with a Roman sword, a cactus, and a fleur-de-lis, all in gold. Below, in the white area, are a red apple with green leaves and the numeral "2" in white.

45. **108th Infantry Regiment (New York National Guard)**

This decorative blue shield is edged in gold. Within this

is a fasces with an ax-head top, supported on either side by lions rampant and gardant, all in gold or yellow color.

46. **109th Infantry Regiment (Pennsylvania National Guard)**
This decorative shield has gold at the top and blue below. In the gold area appear six fleurs-de-lis in blue. Below in the blue, and to the left, is a sheathed Roman sword. To the right is a cactus bush (both in gold). Below the shield a scroll in gold bears the motto *"Cives Arma Ferant"* ("Let the Citizens Bear Arms").

47. **111th Infantry Regiment (Pennsylvania National Guard)**
A blue oval, edged in gold, with a reproduction of a statue of Benjamin Franklin, facing front and in gold.

48. **114th Infantry Regiment (New Jersey National Guard)**
A white shield with a blue saltier cross centered. Above it is a blue and gray Korean *tah gook* from the shoulder insigne of the Twenty-ninth Division, and below it is a blue four-leaf clover. Below this is a scroll with the motto *"In Omnia Paratus"* ("Prepared in All Things").

49. **119th Infantry Regiment (North Carolina National Guard)**
This squared shield has within it a ferocious lion rampant. The whole is divided equally; half blue, and half white. The top is blue and the lion white; below, the combination is reversed. At the bottom is a scroll with the motto "Undaunted" in blue.

50. **121st Infantry Regiment (Georgia National Guard)**
An old-style gray bonnet with blue ribbon and bow.

51. **123rd Infantry Regiment (Illinois National Guard)**
A shield of blue, edged in white; within this is a winged dinosaur, also in white. Below this is a scroll in blue, with the motto "1-2-3-Go" in white.

52. **126th Infantry Regiment (Michigan National Guard)**
This is a white shield with a blue saltier centered upon it. In each angle is a fleur-de-lis in blue. Below this is a scroll in white with the motto *"Courage sans Peur"* ("Courage without Fear").

53. **135th Infantry Regiment (Minnesota National Guard)**
A white shield with a blue saltier centered on it. Above it

42

43

44

45

46

47

48

49

50

51

52

53

54

55

56

57

58

59

60

61

is a fleur-de-lis and below is a bovine skull; to the left is a figure "8" and to the right are crossed bolo knives, all in red. Within the saltier is a three-leaf clover in white and within this is a trefoil in blue. Below the shield is a scroll with the motto "To the Last Man" in blue.

54. **140th Infantry Regiment (Missouri National Guard)**

A blue shield edged in gold, with a wide band of gold. Within this are two crosses of Lorraine, also in blue. Below and to the left is a six-pointed star from the Seventh Corps Badge of the Civil War. This is in white, edged in gold.

55. **142nd Infantry Regiment (Texas National Guard)**

This blue shield with a wide wavy band of red in the center has at the top of it a shell-torn church steeple of Saint-Étienne, France, in white. Below this on a scroll is the motto "I'll Face You."

56. **145th Infantry Regiment (Ohio National Guard)**

A white shield, with a wide, blue wavy bend design. At the upper or right corner is a falcon in black, and in the lower area is a giant cactus in green.

57. **153rd Infantry Regiment (Arkansas National Guard)**

A blue shield with a wide wavy bend in white, edged in gold. At the upper right is a fleur-de-lis in white, and at the lower left is a cactus in white. Below is a scroll with the motto "Let's Go."

58. **156th Infantry Regiment (Louisiana National Guard)**

A shield, the upper half in blue with a white saltier within it. The lower section is white, with a leopard gardant in blue taken from the arms of Normandy, France. Below this is a blue scroll with the motto *"Dieu et Moi"* ("God and I") in white letters.

59. **158th Infantry Regiment (Arizona National Guard)**

A blue shield, edged in gold; within it a gila monster in gold. Below the shield, in a blue scroll edged in gold, is the motto *"Cuidado"* ("Take Care") in gold.

60. **165th Infantry Regiment (New York National Guard)**

A green shield, edged in gold; in the center bend is a rainbow in full colors. At the right and above is a red three-leaf clover edged in gold, from the Second Army Corps Badge of the Civil War. Below and to the left is the cap device of the regiment in 1851, a shield with the numeral "69" in black. It has a trefoil at the top of the shield, and this in turn is supported by two Irish wolfhounds. All this is in gold.

61. **166th Infantry Regiment**
This white shield has a wide blue inner border and is edged in white. Within the shield is a rainbow of varied colors. Below the rainbow is a black Maltese cross, and below the shield is a scroll with the motto "Follow Me" in blue.

62. **174th Infantry Regiment (New York National Guard)**
This shield has a red cross saltier centered in it. The shield is white, and superimposed upon the saltier is a large fleur-de-lis in white. At the left is a castle of Spanish design in red; at the right is some cactus in green.

63. **180th Infantry Regiment (Oklahoma National Guard)**
This blue shield has three arrows arranged like a pyramid, in silver. Above the shield is a wreath in white and blue, and above this is the head of an Indian warrior in full dress war bonnet. Below the shield is a scroll in silver with the motto *Tanap Nanaiya Kia Alitaiyaha* ("Ready in War or Peace") in blue.

64. **181st Infantry Regiment (Massachusetts National Guard)**
A decorative blue shield, edged in gold, with a Colonial powderhorn and hanger in the center.

65. **184th Infantry Regiment (California National Guard)**
A shield in blue, edged in gold, with a wide gold chevron in the center. Above this, and at the left, is a battle ax. To the right is a giant cactus, and below this is a fleur-de-lis, all in gold.

66. **185th Infantry Regiment (California National Guard)**
This blue shield, edged in silver, has in the upper left a silver square with a chevron in blue. Below this is a fleur-de-lis in blue. Below the shield is a wreath with the motto *Numquam Non Paratus* ("Never Unprepared").

67. 188th Airborne Infantry Regiment

A blue shield with a golden sword of freedom, winged in silver, severing a chain, also in silver. Below this is a scroll bearing the motto "Winged Attack" in blue letters on white.

68. 200th Infantry Regiment (Alabama National Guard)

This shield has the top half in gold with a Polynesian war club in red. The lower section is blue, with a silver cross of St. Andrew edged in gold. Below this is a scroll of gold with the motto *"Crede et Vince"* ("Believe and Conquer") in blue letters.

69. 207th Infantry Battalion (Alaska National Guard)

This is a white shield with four lines of blue, two at either side of an anchor, which is also of blue and is centered, flukes down.

70. 224th Infantry Regiment (California National Guard)

This white shield has in the upper lefthand corner a blue square with a white chevron and a fleur-de-lis in white. In the center of the shield is the head of a carabao in blue, recalling the Philippines. Below the shield is a scroll with the motto *"Perseverentia Triumphat"* ("Perseverance Triumphs").

71. 279th Infantry Regiment (Oklahoma National Guard)

A blue shield with a wide white bend across it. Within this are two lightning bolts in red, and in the upper right is a fleur-de-lis in silver. Below the shield is a blue scroll, with the motto "Movin' On."

72. 289th Infantry Regiment

A white shield, with an acorn, grapes, grape leaf, and fleur-de-lis, all in blue. Below the shield is a scroll in white with the motto *"Vincere aut Mori"* ("To Conquer or to Die").

73. 299th Infantry Regiment (Hawaiian National Guard)

A shield, half white and half blue, separated by a wavy border of silver, with the blue at the bottom. Above in the white, a feather helmet of Hawaii in red; below this a blue scroll with the motto *"E Makaala Kakou"* ("Let's Be Alert") in white.

62

63

64

65

66

67

68

69

70

71

72

73

74

75

76

77

78

79

80

81

74. **304th Infantry Regiment (New Hampshire Army Reserve)**
A half blue, half white shield, edged in gold. The upper half is blue behind a charter oak tree in green. Below this is a blue ribbon with "Forward" in gold.

75. **321st Infantry Regiment (North Carolina Army Reserve)**
A white shield with a blue bend diagonally across the center. Within this are two silver fleurs-de-lis. The upper right has a pine tree branch and a pine cone. Below and to the left is a standing wildcat in red. Below the shield is a scroll with the motto *"En Avant"* ("Forward") in black.

76. **336th Infantry Regiment (Ohio Army Reserve)**
A decorative blue shield with a centered fleur-de-lis in white. Below this is a scroll with the motto *"Vincere est Vivere"* ("To Conquer Is to Live").

77. **338th Infantry Regiment (Illinois Army Reserve)**
A shield, white at the top and blue below. In the white is a thistle in green, and below is a scroll with the motto *"Marchons"* ("Let Us March On").

78. **339th Infantry Regiment (Wisconsin Army Reserve)**
A blue shield, edged in gold. The base is white like an ice floe and standing upon this, facing left, is a polar bear in white. The upper lefthand corner is gold with three black birds and a black band from the coat of arms of Cadillac. Below the shield, is a scroll in gold with the motto, in Russian, "The Bayonet Decides," or "We Finish with the Bayonet." This is because the regiment served in the North Russian Expeditionary Force in 1918 and 1919.

79. **350th Infantry Regiment**
A shield with a wide bend diagonally across the front in white and edged in gold. The upper right area is blue with an ear of corn in gold, and the lower left is red with a fleur-de-lis in gold. Below the shield is a scroll in gold with the motto "Fidelity and Service" in blue.

80. **351st Infantry Regiment**
A decorative shield in blue with three five-pointed stars in white. The larger white star represents the North Star; below this is a white fleur-de-lis.

81. **357th Infantry Regiment**
A blue shield, edged in white. At the top is a white disk with the emblem of the Ninetieth Division in blue centered thereon. Below the center is a broken chevron in white, and at the bottom are two white five-pointed stars. Below this is a scroll with the motto *"Siempre Alerta"* ("Always on the Alert").

82. **358th Infantry Regiment (Texas Army Reserve)**
A blue shield with an embattled center section or wide stripe of gold. Above this is a fleur-de-lis, and below it is a five-pointed star, both of gold. Below the shield is a scroll with the motto *"Peragimus"* ("We Accomplish").

83. **370th Armored Infantry Battalion (Old 370th Infantry)**
A blue shield, with a wide white bend, and white lightning bolts at either side, all edged in silver. Below the shield is a scroll with the motto "Power to Strike" in blue.

84. **373rd Armored Infantry Battalion**
This is a blue shield edged in gold, and in the center is a wide wavy fess, or band, of golden orange. Within are a square and a triangle of black. Below the shield is a scroll with the motto "Perform the Task" in black.

85. **376th Infantry Division (Massachusetts Army Reserve)**
A shield with a band or wide diagonal line of red edged in gold, and a golden lightning bolt within it. The upper right area is blue; the lower, gold, with a rattlesnake in black coiled to strike.

86. **385th Infantry Regiment (Rhode Island Army Reserve)**
A golden shield, with a Pilgrim hat, a black hat with a white band and a golden buckle. Through the crown of the hat is an Indian arrow in gold. Below the hat is a scroll with the motto "Follow Me."

87. **389th Infantry Regiment (New York National Guard)**
A blue shield with a gold sunburst and framed in gold.

88. **405th Infantry Regiment (Illinois Army Reserve)**
A blue shield, with a wavy bend, or diagonal line, bordered in silver. Below is a scroll in silver with the motto "Up Front" in blue.

89. **411th Infantry Regiment (Minnesota Army Reserve)**
A shield, half blue and half white, is divided by shapes resembling mountain peaks. In the blue at the top is a rattlesnake in gold. Below and around the shield is a scroll with the motto *"Paratus Ferire"* ("Ready to Strike").

90. **413th Infantry Regiment (Oregon Army Reserve)**
A blue shield, edged in silver, with a sea gull in flight in white. Below the shield is a scroll with the motto *"Fortior ex Asperis"* ("Stronger after Difficulties") in blue.

91. **417th Infantry Regiment (Connecticut Army Reserve)**
A blue shield, framed in silver, with a figure of Nathan Hale, taken from a statue in Hartford, Connecticut. Below the shield is a scroll with the motto "Spirit of '76."

92. **425th Infantry Regiment (Michigan National Guard)**
A white shield with a chevron composed of eleven blue five-pointed stars has in the upper portion a black arrow. A sunburst is toward the front, and near the rear is a palm tree in green. At the bottom is a crowned armed lion in silver and gold. Below is a scroll in silver with the motto "Let the Drum Beat" in blue.

93. **502nd Airborne Infantry Regiment**
A blue shield, edged in gold, has an eagle's claw with talon extended. Below is a scroll in gold, with the motto "Strike" in blue.

94. **503rd Airborne Infantry Regiment**
This white shield has an inverted triangle of blue at the top which merges into a fortress, or a broken fort. In the top area there are three parachutes in white, and the top part of the fort in reverse in white. Below the shield is a scroll of white and blue with the motto "The Rock" in white.

95. **505th Airborne Infantry Regiment**
A white shield, with four bendlets, or diagonal lines, in blue. Superimposed upon this is a winged black panther. Above the shield is a wreath of blue and white above a white cloud. In front is a winged arrowhead, point down and in red. Below the shield is the motto "H-Minus" in blue on a silver scroll.

82   83   84   85

86   87   88   89

90   91   92   93

94   95   96   97

98   99   100

96. 506th Airborne Infantry Regiment

This blue shield, edged in silver, has a white thunderbolt in a bend at the center. Above are six parachutes in silver, and below, near the bottom, is a mountain peak in green. Below the shield is a silver scroll with the motto *"Curr Ahee"* ("Stand alone") in blue.

97. 508th Airborne Infantry Regiment

This is a shield of blue, edged in white, with a white bend and within this a lion passant in red. Below this is a silver and red scroll with the motto "Fury from the Sky" in red.

98. 511th Airborne Infantry Regiment

The upper part of the shield is blue (for the sky) and the lower part is green (for the earth), with a wavy shape for clouds. In the green area to the left are a crossed kris knife and a war club from New Guinea. In white and to the right is a sunburst with rays. Superimposed upon the shield is a wedge, representing a parachute. In white and within this is a torii, or Japanese gateway, in red. Below the shield is a blue scroll with the motto "Strength from Above."

99. 701st Armored Infantry Battalion

At the center this white shield has a raging lion in blue, grasping a golden fleur-de-lis. Behind, in the center, is a wide band of black. Below the shield is a scroll, in silver, with the motto "Gallantly Forward" in blue.

100. 702nd Armored Infantry Battalion

This yellow shield, edged in silver, has within it a ferocious-looking dinosaur in red. Below the shield is a scroll in red with the motto *"Memor Esto"* ("Be Mindful") in yellow.

101. 389th Tank Battalion

This gold shield bears a jayhawk in full color — blue, white, and brown, with a black beak — rising as in flight. Below this is a gold scroll with the motto "Fighting Hawk" in black.

102. 649th Engineer Topographic Battalion

This red shield, edged in silver, has a stadia rod and drafting dividers crossed, in silver. There is a silver scroll below with the motto "Pathfinders" in red.

103. Air Forces Proving Ground Group

This black shield, edged in gold, has the figure of a fictional heraldic monster, an opinicus, in gold. A gold scroll below has the motto "Proof by Trial" in black.

104. Fifth Medical Battalion

This is a shield of red and silver. The red is above with five five-pointed stars in gold. Below them is a gold scroll with the motto *"In Bello Misericordia"* ("Humanity in War") in black.

105. 152nd Signal Company

This is a black disk with a double silver border. Within the disk is an orange hand holding a black and silver horn. Below this is a black scroll with the motto "Resolute to Achieve" in silver.

106. 248th Signal Battalion

This shield, in dark blue and yellow, has an arm and band grasping two thunderbolts (symbolizing signals) in silver. Below this is a scroll of silver with the motto "Always Talking" in black.

107. Headquarters, Eighteenth Wing, Air Force

This trefoil shape is edged in gold. Within it, in full color, a smoking volcano rising from the sea. Superimposed in front is a three-bladed propeller in black.

108. Twenty-first Coast Artillery

This red and gold symbol of heraldry is intertwined in the colors of the artillery (standing for the coastline, for defense). It has red at the top and gold at the bottom in a shield.

109. Eleventh Ordnance Company

The upper part bears a black, early-type ordnance bomb with a red flame at the top, and the numeral "11" in gold. Below is a scroll in gold with the motto *"Peragimus Omni"* in black.

110. Thirty-first Fighter Group — Air Force

This shield has the Air Force colors: orange at the top section, blue at the bottom. Within the orange is a fierce mythical winged animal, the wivern, in blue. The diagonal

101

102

103

104

105

106

107

108

109

110

111

112

113

114

115

116

117

118

119

120

separation line is shaped like a cloud. There is a scroll at the top with the motto "Return with Honor."

111. 760th Transportation Battalion

This red shield bears a diesel locomotive in silver and black with its headlight and beam in yellow, on a silver track. Below this is a silver scroll with the motto *"Recte Ferio"* ("I Strike Straight") in black.

112. 511th Engineer Separate Battalion

This shield is half red and half silver. The silver at the top has a five-pointed star in red within, and below is a silver fleur-de-lis on red.

113. 321st Cavalry Regiment

A brown grizzly bear, holding in its paws a green garland of oak leaves and acorns, which is tied with a red ribbon. The bear is standing on a gold scroll, which has the motto *"Tiens Ta Foi"* ("Hold Thy Faith").

114. 601st Tank Destroyer Battalion

A gold square with a Y-shape in black with eight five-pointed stars in gold.

115. Thirtieth Engineer Topographic Battalion

This red shield has a drafting triangle and dividers in silver. Below them is a silver scroll with the motto *"Imprimis"* ("In the First Place") in red.

116. 156th Field Artillery

This shield, edged in gold, is divided in the center by a wide wavy bend of white. The lower left is red, and the upper right blue with a taro leaf and a fleur-de-lis in gold. The upper lefthand corner is a gold square with a red cross of St. Andrew crossed with a blue saltier.

117. 217th Coast Artillery

The shield is red for artillery, with the pile (the wedge shape) in white, representing a searchlight. The upper left-hand quarter is a square edged in silver with a red cross. There is black between the arms, and centered in the cross is a squirrel; above is a five-pointed star; both are in silver. Below the shield is a red scroll with the motto, "In Liberty's Defense" in silver.

118. 462nd Armored Car Squadron

This is a gold shield with a wide gray bend and with smaller dark blue stripes at either side. Superimposed upon this is a stalking black leopard.

119. 308th Quartermaster Battalion

This buff shield has centered in it a dark blue design edged in silver. It has a dark blue square in the upper lefthand corner; within this is a five-pointed star of silver. Below the shield is a scroll in silver with the motto "Pride in Performance" in blue.

120. 761st Tank Battalion

This silver shield has centered in it a black panther's head with white fangs and a red mouth. A silver scroll below the shield has the motto "Come Out Fighting" in black.

BIBLIOGRAPHY

Blakeney, Jane. *Heroes: United States Marine Corps, 1861-1955.*
Washington: Blakeney, 1957

Bunkley, J. W. *Military and Naval Recognition Book.* New York:
D. Van Nostrand, 1943

Gibbons, Cromwell. *Decorations, Campaign and Service Bars.* New
York: U.S. Insignia Company, 1943

Kerrigan, Evans E. *American War Medals and Decorations.* New
York: The Viking Press, 1964

Morgan, J. McDowell. *Military Medals and Insignia of the United
States.* Glendale, California: Griffin-Patterson, 1941

National Geographic Society. *Insignia and Decorations of the United
States.* December 1919, October and November 1943, and rev.
ed., Washington, December 1944

Townsend, Edward D. *Medals and Corps Badges of the Civil War.*
New York: Appleton, 1884

United States Department of the Air Force. *Uniform Regulations.*
Washington

United States Department of the Army. *The Army Lineage Book.*
Washington

United States Department of the Army. *Army Regulations.* Washington

United States Department of the Army. *Officers' and Noncommissioned Officers' Guide Books.* Washington

United States Department of the Navy. *Uniforms, Decorations,
Medals and Badges.* Washington

United States Government Printing Office. "Armed Forces Insignia"
(chart). Washington

United States Navy. *Bluejackets' Manual.* Washington

United States War Department. *Annual Report.* Washington

Williams, Dion. *Army and Navy Uniforms and Insignia.* New York:
Frederick Stokes, 1918

Wyllie, Robert E. *Orders, Decorations and Insignia.* New York: Put-
nam, 1927

INDEX

Most items are indexed according to the numbers within their respective Parts — e.g. "II-26" means that the item is number 26 (both description and illustration) in Part II. In cases where there is no illustration, and therefore no number, the item is indexed by page.

The numerous items under "Civil War Corps" and "Infantry Regiments" will be found in numerical order on the pages cited.

Index

Index

Index

Index

Index

Index

Index

Index

Index

Index

Index